# A World of Change

Hilda Perez

Copyright © 2012 Hilda Perez
All rights reserved.
ISBN:148259157X
ISBN-13:9781482591576

## DEDICATION

I would like to dedicate this book to the most important people in my life. I would like to start with my children. Monique the oldest, she is my proudest and loudest of my four. Janecka the sweetest and kindest daughter a mom could have, she knows my every mood and tunes in to my needs. Alicia my college scholar, she always keeps me in check. She inspires me in ways that rises above the sun. My precious son Alexander Evan Deer the only one of my four that mirrors me in every way he is the son that every mom would be proud to have. My three grandchildren Jizelle, Jonas, and Angelina, they make me feel like a mom again. They are the cream that tops off my life. My two step children Chris and Zoila who are the sugar in my coffee. Last but certainly not least my husband George Perez that married me with my four, it is you my heart beats for.

# A WORLD OF CHANGE

# A WORLD OF CHANGE

## ACKNOWLEDGMENTS

I want to take this opportunity to let my husband know just how much I appreciate his love and support. This poem is for you.

### The Prize

Never did I want to admit that without you I am inadequate
Like a rope of stars
You have surrounded me with the light that hides my scars
You have taken me out of the gutter
Into a shaded path that gave me wings to fly
I fought you tooth and nail
But your love always prevailed
You are my voice of reason
Even at my own treason
You have pulled me out of the quicksand
In more than one way
You are the reason I am what I am today
You are the MMA of my heart
I have fought you in every form of battle
And your cage I could not rattle
The ultimate fighter
Is your title but
the prize
is mine.

# WHEN DIFFERENT BECAME DANGEROUS

"Change has come," is what our charismatic, good looking leader chanted just six short years ago. A world of change was what we all wanted. We "drank the hope and change cool-aid" but when it went down we were left with a bitter taste.

A game of "patty cake" resulted but he did not turn out to be the baker's man. Instead we were rolled, baked, and put in a 300 degree bond pan. Our dough was about to burn the global economy. We were now creeping towards the exit of financial collapse.

War after war paved the way for this world of change. Every aspect of our life was present in his vision of the future from the cameras that watched your every move to the notion that war was peace.

Go back to sleep, the health care system was here to save the day. Everyone will all be covered and treated the same way. In theory that should have been a good thing, but as a dog has a tail, and a bee has its sting, the health care system had designated alarms attached.

Flora and Dave are 'fit to be tied' with all of these changes and try to turn things around in their community. Flora wanted to break out of the bubble that was slowly filling with methane gas.

Flora, a closet New Yorker with slanted brown eyes, brown wavy hair and 130 pounds of pure Puerto Rican attitude, had just arrived home from a stressful 12 hour shift at the hospital. Out of patience, she snapped the whip of hunger; Flora was just about to reduce her husband Dave to a pile of excrement for not having dinner ready.

"Dave, you know that I have not eaten all day it is 6 p.m. and dinner is not ready," screamed Flora.

She takes the matter of cooking dinner into her own hands as she opens and shuts the kitchen cabinets looking for everything she will need to make dinner.

Jonas, who was six years too young, has been crying with no let up because he wants his vinegar flavored potato chips. Dave was just about to give him the chips just to keep him quiet.

Flora yelled, "Why don't you just act like a dad and get the switch that I took off of the tree and crack him on the buttocks; just don't leave a welt we don't want to give children and families an excuse to take him away. Although, it might be a blessing we barely have enough food to feed two let alone three."

Jonas stopped his crying and replaced the sound of his tears with the annoying bouncing of his make shift basketball; he was getting on her last nerve.

Flora yells out, "Jonas if you don't want your little red ball to be relieved of the air that has wrecked my nerves, you had better take the bounce out of that ball."

Jonas once again burst into an uncontrollable fit of tears that sends his parents into an emotional lather that was assured to exonerate one of them in a court of law. Flora and Dave both wanted to exterminate one another and Jonas has just added fuel to their fire.

Flora's coarse voice lingered in the air as it carried across the sparsely filled room that at one time was filled with priceless antiques. Now all that were left are silent walls and empty rooms. They can thank the down turn in this K-mart economy, and the loss of Dave's job as a welder at the ship yard for their new appreciation of being marked down. One yard sale after another has relieved them of their once superficial past. Now when Flora lost her temper her screams would shatter her families' nerves.

She snapped out once more, "We need milk for the sauce, go over to the Forest house and get me a cup."

Dave's darting voice yelled back, "Last time I checked, I was the man of the house. You go I have to help Jonas with his homework."

Flora's mood was a bit menacing at this point. She was so ready to lay one on him. Fortunately for Dave the only thing left to cook for dinner was in it.

Flora's rolls her eyes and slams her fist on the checkerboard counter top. She became possessed by her rage. Flora roars out, "Well if you want dinner to burn I guess I can go get the milk. We have a credit with Caroline Forest; she borrowed a cup yesterday so we are entitled to barter today. Oh! and if you think that you are going out of this house with your pants hung past your underwear looking like a lazy gangster, you had better clear your brain leaves."

Dave replied, "Well darling I would, but you traded my last belt to Harry Dent."

"Oh! That's right—here take this bungee cord it will stretch around your waist," Flora sheepishly heckled.

Dave rolled his big blue eyes to relieve her from his choke hold look. He then replied, "I am not going to expose myself to being the neighborhood topic for jokes, just give me that left over rope on the floor next to you."

Dave began to tie the laces of the steel toe boots that once earned him some much needed self-respect. He stopped mid-stream as he was tying his last boot string. The delay reaction of his sensitive switch had now turned on. He realized that Flora made him feel like tortured matter the second she walked into the door.

Dave looked like he had a pole shift in his emotional state and said, "You know the word 'please' is still in the dictionary. It would carry a lot of appreciation with me these days."

Flora was not in the mood for his sarcastic sentiments. She took a deep breath and softly replied, "Really Dave I don't mean to be short, but I just got home from a day of sweating over bed pans and incredibly fowl people all day. You know that nurses now have to do all of the work that the CNA's used to do, due to the cut backs in the hospital's budget. I know that I come across like a howling wolf from the moment that I walked through the door, but you could have started dinner over an hour ago. You have been home all day and you know that I work 12 hour shifts and when I get home dinner is not ready. My kettle has been on high steam all week, the least you can do is to make sure that I eat a decent meal. Please, go so that I can finish dinner."

Dave finished tying his shoes and said, "I'll go just to get away from you and the little siren. You might want to take the pot off of the stove until I get back. You know that Jerry is also a house hub, since his cash cow landscaping business got crushed by all of these crazy new environmental regulations. He is going to want to chat a bit about his newly planted garden."

Flora yelled out, "Don't mess with me anymore or I am going to have to hurt you! I'll give you 'five' and I mean that in minutes don't take any longer I am famished!"

Dave opened the door to leave the house when a strange sound to the air overcame the neighborhood. There was a screeching sound like thunder mixed in with rushing water invading our airspace. There was no rain, and as far as he knew no water dams were nearby. The sound seemed to be getting closer as he started his walk down the street. Dave looked up and saw what that clash of sound waves brought in. It resembled a large combination helicopter/washing machine. Dave had never seen anything so intimidating before today.

"The cleaners," that's what we call the police these days because they are no longer looked at as our protectors. Lately they are more like our oppressors. That hideous machine landed in the backyard of the Forest house. Dave had a choice to make go and find out what was going on, or face Flora the beast. Reason took over and he ran back to the wolves den.

Dave shouted, "Flora come here you're going to want to record this to your memory of mind blows!"

Curiously, Flora walked toward Dave with the pot of unmade sauce in her lotion deprived hand.

"What the tweezers is that?" screamed Flora.

The pot that was settled in her small rough hands fell to the ground with a crash.

"The cleaners have added a new toy to their war on vegetables," yelled Flora.

Dave's puzzled face turned pale and to a picture of Jerry and Caroline that was taken with them last year on Ground Hog's Day as he bellowed, "Poor Jerry they are taking his garden down with that monstrous thing."

A long set of iron tweezers came out of the sides of that thing. It proceeded to uproot all of Jerry's priceless organic carrots, delicious red and green tomatoes, huge cucumbers and nutritious lettuce up-links.

What Dave and Flora would give to go back to the time when this once fanciful neighborhood was carefree? It once was beckoned to be lived in by the prominent nose-upping people of the day whose biggest issue was what kind of flowers would look best in their front yards.

Every house was designed to reflect the unique personality of the dwellers inside. For example Mr. and Mrs. Deer's Palladium style home was a classic temple architecture, reminiscent of the ancient Greeks. When inside you would feel like you had a view to the heavens. The ceilings have stain glass panels that during the day would catch the prisms of the sun's rays and at night the moon and stars would harpoon into its grand marble pillar entrance. It was truly eyelash worthy.

The neighborhoods grandeur of an entrance introduced you to their once superficial community. A feeling of awe overtook all senses as one passed the gates into lavishly planted gardens, and tree lined avenue that went on for miles and miles. The nature trails and boardwalk that lead to the grand garden were displayed with tons of azaleas, carnivorous plants, butter-fly plants, and rock outcrops that laced our little piece of paradise.

Yes, everything seemed to be everlasting and it was as long as the world around us did not catch up with our American dream.

That entrance is no longer what it used to be. The bees have been dying off and so were their powers of life-giving magic that contributed to the earth's magnificent sceneries. They were witnessing the fundamental order of life in degeneration free fall. Now they are the "commoners" that were once the who's who of their day. They were all now at the mercies of the goodness of the people that surrounded them house by house. They are all now faced with the prospects of being part of the planed and planted roots of this global agenda.

Today on the 'Daily Rat Show,' they were disgusted by the new rules for carpooling. The 'Rat Show' was the name for the channel 12 news. They found that it is in their best interest to tune in and see what new offenses they and their global communities will and can be charged with just for breathing in air. The new rules for carpooling would include no less than four people per car. The cars would have to be driven through weigh stations. The contents of the car (the people) must be within ten percent of their weight class. If anyone was over their ratio, they were taken to a weight remission center for whatever amount of time it takes to get them to their regulated 'matter of waist.' The new Environmental Czar has seen fit to regulate humans as part of 'Earth's natural resource.'

People were classified as the dying indifference of the planet, in other words 'environmental toilet paper' that should be discarded after use. People have already consumed too much of earth's resources and space, so therefore, the cut backs were for the well-being of the earth that was on an unsustainable course of self-destruction.

"Dave I think you better stay out of the car for at least one month. You are overweight by 20% and we cannot afford to have Jonas taken to the after school mind-control classes. You will have to ride the bike everywhere," sighed Flora.

"Flora, let me ask you something," said Dave.

"My ears are still working Dave ask on," replied Flora.

Dave questioned her with deep concern in his voice," I remember you telling me about a food code that was supposed to go into effect by December, 2009. Could that have something to do with this unnatural weight issue?

Flora put her hands on her head as to prepare herself for what she was about to say. She started her confession with," Yes, darling it did go into effect. The name is "codex alementarius,"and that my love is the real cause of all of the accelerated chronic illnesses people are experiencing worldwide. What's behind codex alementarius? Well, to put it to you gently it is a global program to reduce our over populated earth. The United Nations and the World Health Organization working in conjunction with the multinational pharmaceutical cartel and international banks, all have their hands in this evil program. Its initial efforts in the US with the FDA were defeated, so it found another ally in the FTC. Now Codex, with the FTC and the pharmaceutical alliances, are in control of "Operation Cure-All" to advance their death cult goals.

What are we getting under "Codex?" For starters, low potency dietary supplements that are not useful for therapeutic use. If you want the real life saving supplements you had better have lots of money or are well connected. What is even worse is that common foods such as, garlic, peppermint, herbs, vitamins, minerals, homeopathic remedies, amino acids and other natural remedies that we took for granted most of our lives are now classified as dangerous. They are now classified as drugs because they have therapeutic effects of healing. That is why we are now getting genetically altered food called "GMOS" that are depleted of the vitamins and minerals that we need to sustain normal body functions and weight. Codex has an even more sinister goal and that is to create a world without borders ruled by a virtual dictatorship that is made up of a central bank and multinational corporations. So you see honey that is why so many people are coming in with symptoms of malnutrition and many times severely over weight because of the lack of nutrients in the food. They are eating empty foods that are meant to fill them with all sorts of illnesses. It kills me to have to put these poor souls in the "M" ward and mark their charts "DOA." I guess good things really do come in small packages. I am glad that I have access to the real vitamins and minerals that keep us from falling into the category of the sick and dying.

Dave wondered what that meant, so he inquired in a way not to seem unfamiliar, "Oh! You mean Department of Arrival."

"Cute," replied Flora.

"I wish that was what it meant, but it means something a lot more sinister than that, it means, 'dead on arrival.' " exhaled Flora.

Dave answered with a dejected tone, "but why if they are alive?"

Flora hung her head down low and whispered, "Honey I have to mark their charts that way because they are not going to be treated for their symptoms. They are put in the 'M' ward; 'M' for murder is what it stands for to me, but if you ask anyone else on staff they would have to say 'Malnutrition.'

Dave was beside himself when he realized how much pressure and stress his wife was going through at work. He suddenly grew a face of profound respect and compassion for his wife as he said, "Why did you not tell me what was going on, and how come no one gets in trouble for this horrible injustice?"

Flora looked at Dave with tears in her eyes as she said, "well babe you never asked before and now I wish I never told you. You must not repeat this to anyone or I will get fired. The family members are told that they had internal organ failure and died peacefully. The peacefully part is true. They are given a nice little dose of take me to the moon pills and never wake up. You never get used to writing those three death dealing letters 'DOA.'

"Wow! Honey, I will never give you a hard time when you get home from work again. I am sorry that I was so ridiculous earlier; I guess it has really gotten to me, that I have not been able to find a job and you're shouldering this tremendous load. I wish I would have gone back to school while I collected unemployment. I got into that entitlement state of mind. I thought to myself, I worked all my life I deserve a hand out. After all, I did pay for it out of every pay check that I got for the last twenty years. Now I feel vulnerable to everything and everybody, because I have no control. I need to get my self-respect back. What could I do to make a difference? " asked Dave.

Flora replied, "You have already resolved that problem you have just forgotten. You are being dragged into self-pity. Please, don't do that it shows weakness. We are all doing something very unique and special in our community."

Flora started to write out a check in the name Dave Stroller in the amount of unlimited dollars 100,----------- she then ripped it out and gave it to her husband.

Dave took the checkout of his wife's hand and probed Flora, "Okay! What lesson of the day is this?"

She looked at him and whispered, "No inside meaning to this honey, I just wanted to let you know that your usefulness is limitless. Most communities in this world have fallen off of the humanity tree. You help keep us going by the use of your skills by bartering us a workable life until this crazy new world gets to a better place that is worth living in again. Why, if it was not for you Mr. Beverly would not have had the use of his backup generator that helped sustain his family while their power was out; by repairing his generator you were generating around here and there. Remember we bartered a week's worth of gas that he had stored in his garage before the gas prices sky rocketed. If you would not have had welding skills I would have lost my job, because we did not have the money for gas that week. Don't sell yourself short my love; we have the whole world for that. We need to keep building up one another. Like mountains flowing with water in a desert we need to be."

"Thanks for the confidence talk," responded Dave, as he took her slender hand into his large cracked glove he called his hand.

Dave gently kissed flora's forehead, as he looked at Jonas fast asleep on the couch. He proceeded to pick Jonas up from the couch to put him into bed.

Dave, requested Flora, "Can you flip on the switch of the head lights to his car bed so that he will not sense the darkness of the room and wake up screaming?"

Flora loving remarks, "We might have more past than future, but I love the past that you have given me no matter the time left for our future."

Dave picked up the slim 45 pound child off of the couch and placed him into his car shaped bed.

Flora yawned and stretched her hands up into the air as she lets a tired plea out for Dave to please make sure all of the lights are turned off before coming to bed. She reminds him not to forget to unplug the garage door as well.

"We don't want anyone using a remote to get into the garage; you know that is how the Brooks got broken into last week," Flora bellowed.

As Dave was going to bed he turned his attention to the saying on his wife's pajamas that said, 'rainbows make me smile.' Dave thought to himself, If she only knew that she was the rainbow that made him smile. He suddenly remembered what he was told not to forget, and that was the garage door. So he did what he almost forgot and got into bed to erase the images of that day which will forever be engraved in his long term memory as bizarre.

Sounds of silence filled the room as night broke into morning splendor. The sun barely rose when all of the sudden their hearts were thumped out of a deep sleep with the unexpected sound of a knock at the front door. An intense realism overcame their powers of delusion. Could it be the cleaners? Have they come to get Dave for staring them down the night before? Who could be at the door so early on a Saturday morning?

Flora woke with a start, "my lord what on Earth is going on? Are you going to go and see who it is Dave?" whispered Flora.

"Let's just stay in bed maybe whoever it is will go away," answered Dave.

"I don't want Jonas to wake, I will go and check," replied Flora.

"No! No! We will go together that way we can back each other up, and Flora don't forget the steel bat behind the door" answered Dave.

Windmills of weighty thoughts went through their minds as they approached the door with a touch of vertigo as they suddenly felt sick and paralyzed. Slowly they crack the door open with the chain still on top. Flora stood behind Dave with the bat looking like she was ready to hit one out of the park.

"Who is it? What do you want?" They inquired as one voice.

They both breathed a sigh of relief when they heard Jerry's timid voice.

"Oh! It's just Jerry," they said in unified relief.

"Come on in Jerry," said Dave.

Jerry replied, "I need to make a decision within the next 24 hours that could affect us all. I will be charged with improper use of 'banded and unlawful seed germination.' They want me to give up my source, but if I do I will put our whole system in danger. I don't want the snowball effect to take over us all. One thing will fall into another and we will all get into a windstorm of trouble if they find out what we have been doing. It was a lot more than just seed harboring."

Dave sat unplugged as he shook his head back and forth with his face to the floor; he took a deep breath and groaned as he said, "Gee Jerry talk about being trapped in a hole that sinks at both ends. How much time are they talking about?"

Jerry's eyes began to swell up as he replied, "about two years."

Dave tried to be as an 'ear with a mouth' that has wings as he attempted to give words of support but falls short.

Dave responded, "Jerry honestly I don't know what to say, but you know that we are all guilty of doing one thing or another that is frowned on in this new way of life.

If you fall the dominoes are sure to start on its way to the end and there goes our whole utopia and we will all thread on this thin ice as a whole. As a fellow objector, it is up to you to preserve the integrity of our secrecy. This can be the marble that leads to the downfall of the life line of our survival. I hate to be in your treads. It's you that has been running with the cards and the decks are stacked high," said Dave, as he stumbled to his feet from off of the Victorian style couch.

Flora tries to reverse the heavy feeling in the room by exclaiming, "Jerry if anyone has the back bone it is you. You come from a back ground of uprightness.  Let me remind you how your parents stood firm against Hitler during his reign of terror. They didn't fall into the 'normalcy bias' mentality. They did not leave a good intention behind. Your parents saved 25 Jewish children by placing them in German family homes whom they knew were mirrors of their own ideals. You can actually make a difference to others in there. Those who share with you the custom of the common people will support you, and you them. All of the  hardened criminals are out on the streets helping to raise mayhem in the streets. Why, the Larson's are there for having one of those banned books in their house, I believe it was called' the bible.' Most of the people that are in there are there because of their principles, all of the real criminals are out of their cells and on the streets already. Now, let me make you a cup of coffee and talk about getting our families together for some wholesome up building memories."

Dave Jumped in and injected his encouragement by adding, "I know it is easier said than done, especially when we are not the ones that are going through this dreadful ordeal. We will take care of anything you need done while you are gone. Caroline will not g have to worry about a thing. I will take Karen to and from school. Jonas and Karen can hang out at our house until Caroline gets home from work. As far as the lawn and all of the things that you need done around the house, you know that I am on it."

Jonas gave Mr. Forest a hug and injected his two sense of limited wisdom when he proclaimed in his baby voice, "your last name is perfect, because you can see the forest for the trees and like mom said, you have strong roots. I know I am just a little kid and I don't know much about the world but what I do learn comes from adults like you. You are shaping up my world as much as yours. Me and Karen are in the same school I will walk her to class and make sure that no one makes her feel bad about your absence. Kids can be meaner than grown-ups. Most of them don't have a potty filter. They think since they are small they can get away with saying bad mean things. I am not going to let her fall into the group of kids that are put through that rat-a-tat ringer. After all, I do know karate and I will teach her some moves to make sure she shuts them down fast."

Flora halts her little ninja and tells him to please go and take a shower. Dave walks with Jonas to his room so that Jerry could have some space. Flora gave Jerry a check for $100 dollars she told him to take it for the losses that he just suffered when they took down his garden. He reluctantly took the check and thanked Flora for her kindness.

Jerry looked as if he found himself, and was now ready to take one for the team. When he left the house he yelled out, "I am ready to start cooking the account of my obliviousness."

Incessant thoughts overtook them as a community today. It has been a week since Jerry Forest refused to give up his source of the banned seeds that they as citizens are not allowed to grow. As with antiseptic conditioning they were all assured for the moment that all was fine and it will not be long before their friend was home again. Caroline stood as a university of power as her husband was taken away. We all could benefit from her stealthy manor.

Mr. and Mrs. Larson mentioned earlier in Flora's rendering, of the kind of people that Jerry will encounter has been slated for released from detention next week. They served one year for not turning in their bibles.

Mr. and Mrs. Larson's children have been staying with Mr. Larson's parents so they will be coming home as well. Ironies abound in many ways. The reason why the book was found became wrapped in the conscious of the kids. You see they hated the bible, so they told their 'school sympathizer' who in turn we called the 'SS' which stood for the "snitch squad" to us. The children thought that the 'SS' would just take the book out of the house and that would be the end of its influence that so cramped their sanity. When their parents were taken away they decided to redeem themselves. They took a copy of the bible that was not found, and recorded it to memory. Each took that whole year to put into memory the entire bible, so that between the three of them the bible would still be alive and in their home when their parents returned.

The satires truly abounded in the turnaround in their children's attitudes about the bible and God because as they read the good book they actually developed a real bond with 'All Mighty God.' That was truly a blessing in disguise. Although, they did suffer a flash of darkness being separated from their parents, they became wrapped in the passion of their parent's love of their God in Heaven.

Tonight they were all to welcome them home. Mr. and Mrs. Deer have offered their home for the festivities. There were about 200 people at the home welcoming. No expense was spared to give then a warm painted shade of love party. They arrived on time and the guests were all taken back at what they saw. They both lost so much weight they had hardly recognized them. Besides the weight loss they looked like they were in good spirits. Mrs. Deer raised her hand up as a jester for everyone to please pause for a moment so that Caroline Larson could take the floor and say a few words. Caroline was pale in complection and fragile in form. She was the more outspoken of the two, and took to the honor of saying a couple of words. She looked about the room when suddenly everyone looked like spinning tops.

She took two steps forward leaning as if she was a tower of expression, and all of a sudden she fell to the floor. She was overwhelmed and could not have expressed herself better with any amount of words. Larry Larson made sure his wife was okay and proceeded to do the honors for them both.

He started out with a mild timid voice as he asked for everyone's attention than preceded to say, "Let me humbly and with the voice of a truly thankful heart say that we are truly awe struck by the circle of friends that have lightened our load. The concern and care that was poured out by all of you has touched us to our core. We never thought for a moment that we were not thought of, and for no time were you all not part of our remembrances that carried us through. Thank you for taking care of our home. The lawn looks as good as or better than the day we left. The pool sparkles like the beams of light in your eyes. It was so nice to come home to our immaculately clean home. Tina and Paul I want to extend a special acknowledgment for the care of our extended family Amy and Sugar our loyal fur-kin. I know it was an extra burden to feed and nurture them in the way that they were accustomed. Why by the looks of them they seemed not to be effected by our long detention."

Laughing—to himself louder inside than out—Larry echoed, "The stocks they wanted to put us in to break our wills only strengthen our resolve to be unmoving mules. We live in a world that is longed to be refreshed by the warmth of real smiles that don't carry a knife behind their back. Our life of purpose has not adapted to the changes of other peoples plans. In closing I would like to say we will be back at our family practice to provide medical care so you know where to go to get treatment for all your ills."

That was truly an inspirational speech; their eyes could not hold back the fountain of joyful tears that streamed forth from every eye in attendance. As a matter of fact, they feel more convicted to their cause than ever before. That was the super glue needed to bond them all to a principle of what was pure and true.

Caroline and Larry Larson are both doctors. They had their own practice and were more than ready to go back and start attending to the medical needs of their community. They were told by their staff of member doctors that the new standards of their practice had changed in that year. The 'complete lives system' mandated that they fill out forms on each patient that had signs of physical or mental limitations to the 'soaps' which stood for Severely Over Apprehensive People Syndrome. You see, under that program the doctors would issue the papers, or more like "orders," to pick up the defective units (people) to their new home in the new 'Medical Deficiency's Facility,' where the pickled face tarts that run the place would decide the fate of their good organs. Yes, 'organs.'

They were going to be used as replacement parts for the people we now called the 'empty pits of the living' because they only cared about themselves at other peoples expenditure. That was not going to happen on their watch. All of their patients were perfect and those forms will just have to sit on the shelf and collect dust. They plan on doctoring their patients and curing the disease of discontent of what they call 'passivity.'

As a matter of fact, Mr. Larson told people to remove 'organ donator' from their driver's license. He told them that people were targeted and set up to die in what looked like accidents so that people with money did not have to be on a waiting list for rare organs that could take years to find a perfect match. The rich pay millions for a healthy heart, something that they all lack. They made sure that they did not die until they could harvest the fruits of their wickedness. Eva, one of his healthy Olympic hopefuls was targeted for her liver. The unwilling victim had been incarcerated on a fake drug charge. Her tissue compatibility was systematically analyzed and matched as a perfect fit for an over indulging drunk with deep pockets that were lined in her blood. He termed it 'organ surfing' since they look for healthy organs such as kidneys, hearts, pancreas, liver, cornea and even skin from the highest quality.

This morning our persona sirens were louder than they have been in weeks. Everybody was awakened by their cell phone's new powers over their lives. What was once such a cool convenience, and the smarter the phone the better, was now their 'personal monitoring device,' not so good to have anymore. All of the cell phones, even the ones turned off, were active simultaneously. An announcement was made that said the following:

"This is a public announcement all regulated citizens are to report to their 'common stupor' supervisory leader and report any and all new suspicious activity. All credible information will afford you extra food coupons."

Everyone quietly got up and followed their mind numbed orders. We had no fear of our supervisory leader that in the not-so-old-days was called the home owner association president.

Mr. Cart's had coffee and donuts for everyone. He sent in the monthly 'snitch report' that read, "Nothing to report in this sector." After his faxed transmission the neighbors all just sat around and used the time together to catch up on each other's lives.

Larry Larson shouted into his monitoring device, "nothing to hear here," a silence loomed over the room. They knew that he was never going to be taken off of the 'POCS list' which stood for People on Constant Surveillance; he was always listened to. They were afraid that he was doomed to get into trouble for his brazen attitude with his new found freedom.

Mr. Carts put on the smooth jazz station to lighten the mood and everyone sat down to decompress. What a travesty to have to live on the edge and be forced to talk in code so that you will not be dragged into a not so necessary conflict with your elected overlords.

"Dave how is the job search?" asked Ben.

"Well I have an 'examination' to go on tomorrow," replied Dave. That is what interviews are called these days because people are being picked over like cattle now. There are so many people looking for work, you almost have to be in someone's pocket to get a good paying job. A fact that is even sadder is the college students. Their higher education has been discarded as negate, reducing them to server's positions instead of the ones to be served.

"I noticed that you rode your bike everywhere for the past month. I rather enjoyed the basket with wheels that you have cleverly attached to your bike to take Jonas back and forth in," smiled Ben.

"Yup, Jonas's skateboards come in handy," laughed Dave.

"Okay, Okay let's stop having fun and get down to today's community business," interrupted Ben, as he announced that as of today the water usage reports have come in well above satisfactory. "I am very proud of all of your effects in the reuses of our water supply. Oh! and before you all go let me remind you that tomorrow the sky will be green," stated Mr. Cart.

They all knew that 'green skies' meant that there were city inspectors coming to check on how 'green efficient' their homes are. They all took the time to switch back the banned light bulbs to the mandated pigtail light bulbs. They knew that the pigtails were a sneaky way to 'soft kill' us through the mercury that they contained. Cancer has been up drastically and they were cutting back on our "indulgent murder" numbers. It was just another way to control population without being down right obvious. They are ahead of the game and are grateful for the risk that Ben takes to keep them safe from a world of "when different became dangerous."

It has been one month since the Wonder sisters have graduated from school. Doris and Phillip are very proud of their twin girls. They have managed to keep themselves out of the 'elite training camps' for the 'youth global elite soldier program. The program was designed to give youth from ages 12 to 25 a chance to join this 'under achievers' reign of power trip. They didn't want the kids that had GPA'S higher than 1.5. They made sure that they keep their grades up and showed the system that they were productive citizens. It's not clear why they are called the 'elite youth' when only the students with failing grades and low IQ's are being taken. They were viewed as the 'perpetual adoration' of their society. What a contradiction in plain sight. They were control freaks with a gun. Do we need any more validation of the term 'when different became dangerous?'

Everybody is going to miss the girls because as a safety measure they have all got together to send them to China to work for Mr. Wang's sister in her clothing factory. Yes, that sounds backwards.

Our free society is sending their prize possessions to a Country that's used to be the role model of control, another Paradox of everyone's new underappreciated life; and yet, Just another example of "when different became dangerous.'"

Everyone would rather be safe than sorry for in most places in our neck of the world there seemed to be a competitive market for suffering.

Alvin Hicks who was a retired cop was taken to jail for his comments about gun control that he posted on his Face Page status. A 'Snatch team' showed up at his house within hours. In the presence of his two teenage sons he was thrown to the floor. While 'the snatch team' called him a terrorist even though they were the ones doing the terrorizing. Flora and Dave had no dog in this hunt so the outcome of this issue was not a pressing matter that consumed their concern. None the less, it was something that kept coming up among their friends that would turn into a keg fire of "TNT" filled words that would kill their peaceful get-togethers.

Last week the public was charged another two percent of their already strained paychecks for new taxes that were supposed to be put on the rich people; but just like everything else they were promised, it seemed to be 'thrown up' on the backs of the middle class that were slowly being hot pressed between the rich and poor slowly flattening their bread.

Betty was upset when she got her first paycheck. Flora saw her this morning while on one of her runs. Betty chases Flora to show her something. Flora stops out of respect for her need to vent but she was a talker and Flora knew her workout was done at this point.

"Happy new year of taxes," Betty said in a rant.

"Look at this check that is my truck payment, or a week's worth of groceries. My kids can forget about ever going to see a movie again. I don't know about you but this is significant for me. While the 'fiscal cliff' compromise spared the rich, most of us poor working class slobs have an increase in our income taxes.

Did you notice that your payroll taxes for Social Security and Medicare have just chewed away another layer of our meager remunerations? This whole deal is a joke, as a matter of fact; our rising health care premiums and the ongoing furloughs are only lining the pockets of the haves who just received a pay raise on our flipsides. I was happy that I got a pay raise of 2% but that was done away with and then some. Let me tell you Flora, I feel like a sheep that was invited to eat dinner with two lions. Well, we sheep should have known better and not taken their invitation," exhaled Betty.

Flora had to stop Betty or she was never going to get to work on time. She cleared her throat as a signal for Betty to get some air as she compassionately admonished her situation and said, "I got the same bump but what can we do? We have been bum rushed and that is a fact, but the royals have had the red carpet spread out since the beginning of time. To be honest with you I am tired of these economic wolf cries that are falling on deaf ears. They need to take their foot off of the money printing pedal but that was not going to happen until they hit the financial brick wall. I get so upset when I start to think about this subject; so let's end this conversation with my invite to dinner and a movie night at my house. Our families could use some good bubbles that pop wet not dry.

Why don't you come over tonight and we will rent a movie together. We don't need to go out to a movie let's have a good time and take the wind out of the storm that wants to hit us where it hurts. Don't make it hurt make it work. So come to my house at 8 p.m. and I will have your favorite caramel popcorn. I just picked up the last two at the 'Slash A Buck store'," replied Flora.

Betty's mood softened and she agreed to come at 8 p.m. She than asked if Jonas could please come over for a sleep over afterwards. Her son Allen just got off of punishment and he wanted to spend some time with Jonas. Flora agreed and they went their separate ways. As Flora jogged back home she suddenly realized that this tax thing boomeranged from the 1% to the 99% is another great example of, "when different became dangerous."

# A World Of Change

Today Dave had to pick Jonas up from school after his poor baby was interrogated for three hours by his tubby love handle principle, Mrs. Love Joy. He brought a toy Sponge crab bubble gun to school. He was charged with attacking his classmates with detergent. His sentence was three days of out of school suspension. Poor Jonas was put through the wringer for an innocent act of floating suds. This is just another extreme case of, "when different became dangerous."

Today there was quite uproar over the organic foods "GMO" deception that turned Mr. Adams into a hard-hitting ram when he flooded every light pole and store window with the truth of what was being fed to people and animals as nutritious. It is like having organic spies in their bellies that are sabotaging their health. GMO stands for genetically modified food. This is what his flyer said: "You are being bio-teched with seeds that will kill you. Educate yourself or you will wind up a warning symbol as well."

While he was putting up his last flyer he was subdued by what looked like a toy airplane that released a dart meant to put his lights out making it easy for the "cleaners" to take him in. He was a wanted 'information terrorist' that went underground. They were waiting for the gopher to pop his head out of his hole and when he did his goose was cooked. Later on the Channel 12 News he was regarded as 'black mold' that spread infectious ideas which lead to turret activities and he was therefore labeled, a public hazard.

"I am not the only squirrel that was chewing on that acorn of knowledge, I had better watch my step or I will end up the same way," thought Flora.

Dave yells out, "Isn't that the guy that you used to listen to on the internet radio?"

"Yes, I was wondering what happened to him. He had a huge following. I can guarantee his followers are not going to take this with their eyes padlocked. There will be trouble. I stopped listening to him because he was making me nervous. I am already neurotic. I did not need any more help in the furthering of that part of myself," replied Flora.

Early the next morning Flora is furious at Dave for calling her she-man. He always made fun of her every time she came out with bleach on her upper lip. Flora was researching some information on the 'NDAA' when Dave started his taunt.

He then adds to the insult when he says, "Hey she-man why are you looking up that information? You sat there a couple of days ago and said that you were done with that because it made you nuts. So why are you doing it now? I am going to have to send you to information rehab."

Flora threw her lap top computer at him and missed. She realized how foolish that was because now she had to buy another one.

Dave laughs and says, "You know honey it should have been you that was required to take 28 weeks of anger management. That little temper tantrum is going to set us back a few bucks that we don't have."

Flora did not respond she just put on her coat and headed to the store to purchase another laptop. As she was leaving she says, "Because you enjoy ticking me off so much I took your 18kt Gold 'Dave bracelet.' I am going to a cash-for-gold store. This thing is worth at least $2,000 with the price of gold so high now. Thank you for my new laptop honey." Flora had a smile from ear to ear as she shut the door.

Dave ran to the room to see if she really had the "grapefruits" to do that to him. He shuffled though his underwear drawer to find the only valuable asset he had left. He had saved it from her clutches for over five years now. She sold everything and anything on ZBay to make extra money. He had no problem with that he knew she was a go getter and he loved that about her, but she has gone too far this time. While she was gone he decided that for the first time he was going to get even with her. He took his shaving cream and put it inside of all of leather purses and shoes. He then lined them all up by the front door so that when she comes in she would trip over her precious shoes. She was going to get a taste of her own venom.

Flora came in after an hour with a new laptop computer. Just as she was about to call out for Jonas to help her with some bags, she tripped over the shoes that Dave stacked up by the front door. She saw that they were bathed in shaving cream but she did not even bat an eyelash at him. Dave did a double-take to make sure it was her that walked in.

She just laughed at him and said, "Dave you are really an amateur at being vindictive. I don't even care about those shoes anymore. I was going to sell them on ZBay next week. You should have used pudding that would have made me mad. Oh! by the way thanks for cleaning them. I use your shaving cream to clean the bath tub when I run out of Ajax." Flora digs into her purse and takes out his 'Dave bracelet' as she brandished it into the air she yells out, "Sucker!"

Dave feels small not only because his wife has just smashed him like a bug as she so often does, but mostly because she didn't sell his bracelet and she got a coke out of him—something he always told her that she was not going to be able to do and she just did.

He looked at her and said, "How did you pay for that computer?"

Flora yelled out, "My Best Buy plastic still works; it was my fault that I let you get to me. Besides, I have to learn how to control my impulse to take things out on you. You might want to find a better hiding place for that. You never know when my evil side will want to cash it in."

Dave took the bracket out of her hand and confessed, "I know I love you because it is times like these that I will look back on and laugh at myself. The only thing that I will never laugh about is the time that you put dirt in our food because you were angry at us for moving some of your precious antiques into the garage when we first moved into the house. That one still hurts. You just sat there and laughed at us as we crunched away on our favorite beef and potatoes stew that you made with so much flavor. But till this day it goes down in lumps of bad feeling of your cunning ways. I do love you God knows I do."

"Look you knew that I was in therapy when you met me. I practically had a warning sign around my neck that read 'deadly.' I am getting better give me some credit," snapped Flora.

Jonas interjected and said, "Mom you should wear a real sign that says 'crazy person about to invade your space.' I love you mom but you have to stop driving me and dad to the 'time out corner' of our mind. You don't want me to wind up a little twisted like you and a lot disturbed like dad."

"I will promise to start a count to 10 from now on. Can't we all just get ready for our guest? So chill out. Now that you both just reminded me of my psychosis I would like to get things ready for a fun time," said Flora.

Flora was not in the mood for anymore drama but for some reason she could not turn off the news that was just breaking. The reporter could barely contain himself as he tried to restrain himself from bursting into laughter.

The channel 12 reporter started out with, "Today people from a local church are being taken up, but not in the way that they would like to be. You see they are just the latest perpetrators of the hate speech treaty that outlaws any kind of defamation against persecuted groups of people. What kind of speech could possibly be defined as hate coming from a church?" was his comment as he continued to explain who was doing the taking of these poor souls.

It was the 'cleaners,' they were cleaning up the unwanted dirt left behind in the, "hate speech overhaul." There was a rat among them at the service that was recording the service over his smart phone.

They waited for key words to be said. The preacher went on to talk about the subject of gay marriage. Well, 'gay' was a ding word. Not five minutes later the sky came alive with the sound of the "Octo-choppers" in the air. They were quite interesting to look at. They had eight hands on each side of the chopper. There were a total of five that surrounded the area. The unknowing preacher was now silenced when he heard a blow horn of a voice blasting orders from outside.

What was said sent every cat inside running from the rat in their mist. They were ordered to come out with their hands up and their mouths shut. They were now guilty of violating the "hate speech treaty" and they were all to be arrested. You should have seen those choppers in action. They were scooping up the people with their tentacles and body cuffing them. Yes, you can say that it is all over for anyone or any group that talks about controversial organization in a negative way. Their society of rats is clearing out the kitty boxes of the cats that refuse to be hushed. The rats get the cats now don't that just reek of, "when different became dangerous."

Betty is now renting out rooms in her house to help pay for their basic needs. I don't think that they will have a problem filling the rooms. So many people are living in their cars or in make shift tents. Although many people are returning to work, they are often taking jobs with lower wages and less job security.

"Good-morning," Betty groaned Flora as she put out the trash before garbage management came.

"What's so good about it?" replied Betty.

"I see you're in as good of a mood as I woke up in, I see you have some new cars in your driveway. Did you get some new tenets?" Smiles, Flora.

"Yes, but they have two kids and you know how much I like kids Carl fell in love with the little darlings so she made me do it. I should have let her have one when she was in child bearing prime. We were too busy making money and acquiring wealth and now I say for what? At least, you don't have to rent out rooms just to stay above the grid," Betty answered.

Flora laughed and started to do the thing that she does when she thought something was too much for her to handle at that moment. Flora has a nervous tick that helps her transform her state of mind by passing one hand up and down past her face three times just in case the 1st and 2nd attempts fail. She responds to Carl with sarcasm as she says, "If you call working six days a week 12 hours a day and living on peanut butter and jelly five out of the seven days a week good, than we are doing great."

Carl feels bad and redeems himself by saying, "I forgot Dave still has not found a job. I wish I could help but we are letting go of people this week. The company is avoiding the new taxes from the healthcare bill so we are shaving off ten employees to make sure that we have no more than forty-nine. I have to do the work of three people now. Tell him to go apply online they are hiring for internment officers. I know that sounds horrible but it will put food on the table."

"Carl you go home and beat yourself for that suggestion. You know that we have friends in there, besides you have to pass the fluoridated brain test to see if you are crazed enough to be accepted for the position. Dave would never pass," shouted Flora.

"I forgot myself for a moment I am so sorry. Please don't take what I said to heart I am not thinking clearly," replied Carl as he got in his car to go to work.

"Don't worry yourself all is good between us. Have a better day than you are allowed to have," waved Flora as she went back into the house.

The new job postings are on the "pacified news" website. Dave was up and looking as he made his wife coffee to go because she was now running late for her shift. His last interrogation did not go so well. He was desperate and was now willing to clean dump sites or pick fruit, anything would not be beneath him at this point in his life.

Today was the day that all odd number addresses are allowed to go to the grocery store to pick up the foods that has been rationed such as potatoes, fruit and coffee. So off Flora goes to pick up their rat bites. There was a new reward plan that kicked in today. Anyone with information leading to the exposure of any hidden and secret activities that are banned by regulation gets double portions. Flora knows people that will turn in their own mothers in to get more "GMO" rations.

While there Flora ran into Yeti, one of their neighbors who are the pharmacist at the store.

"Yeti, how have you been? How come you did not come to the graduation party for the twins," asked Flora.

"I have been working overtime on all this new paperwork that has to be filled out even for the over the counter medicines. I am not even getting paid overtime I just am expected to do it all before my shift is over or I work for free," Yeti replied.

Yeti was filling out those very forms while she talked to Flora.

"Sorry I cannot give you eye contact Flora but I don't want to work for free today. Did Dave get a job yet Flora?" Yeti asked.

"No, he is still looking," responds Flora.

"Well I have some work that we need done around the house. Can you ask Dave to call Tom so we can get it done?" asked Yeti.

"For sure Yeti, I will have him call when I get home. We will do the usual trade, you know what that is. Yes, no need to give an ear full to the flies on the walls," laughed Flora.

The next day Flora and Dave were looking forward to a day in the sun walking on the boardwalk shaded by the loving leaves' tree branches; Dave noticed something out of the ordinary.

"Flora what is wrong with that picture?" asked Dave.

"That was not a picture that was the "phantom of the Not-tra" which means "not really going on," said Flora.

They could not of had imagined how horribly wrong this day was about to go, but they are not going to be allowed to turn back and have no consequence. They just stepped into what was called "looking for manmade solutions you can expect man made mud." The water was being drained out of our man made pond. Flora let go of Dave's hand and she picked up a rock to throw it at the pop belly official looking man who was about to be in their face.

"Either you folks cannot read or you're made out of some unusual sand," said the bloodsucker that was draining their water.

"Well, excuse me sir but we live in this community we were not made aware of the travesty that we are witnessing. Besides, you are on private property and you should not be here. We have every right to what we paid for!" yelled Flora as she stood with her hands on her hip in a defendant position.

"Well, little missy you being no bigger than a corn nugget, I must say I admire your sand talking to me in such a tone!" yelled the obstinate old coot.

"Well, let me just educate you fine folk on what is called the, 'Tame project.' We have taken claim to this land by default. Any land with water larger than the size of a puddle is now government property. The land will be given back to the original inhabitants and it was not you. I mean animals that were here before humans.

We are going to make this whole community a flat land very soon," bragged the gunk face man as he puts chewing tobacco into his mouth.

Dave looked at him with eyes of knives, as he angrily proclaimed his disapproval of the project, "We will be filing a formal lawsuit to stop this disturbance. We will not just sit back and take this. We have laws that protect our property rights."

"Whatever helps you sleep at night dude, but for now you folks will have to leave this area and go about your business out of here," stated the fowl faced old coot.

They are all for animal rights but this has gone far beyond what was acceptable. There are already 50 acres of conservation around them. That is why they choose to live here. This was by far the worst travesty of, "when different became dangerous."

Everyone needs to ban together tighter than ever. She was going to have to give everyone here a stronger cup of espresso to wake them up to what was in progress. Everyone all needs to come together for the purpose of united we stand divided we fall.

They are in the middle of what is called "sibling rivalry rearing its ugly green snout." The green agenda is about to divide us even further into this battle of "we need to do it for the earth." They do agree they need to take care of the earth and they always do their part, but this agenda was a great cover to grab more control and not to make the world a better place to live and breathe in.

Flora says talks out loud "If I was God I would evict 90% of us because we have all trashed his beautiful planet, but this yoke of taxes and regulations are taking away our way of life. The American Indians had it right. They believed in the balance of man and nature. If we would have learned just one thing from them, that should have been it. It looks like we are and were always the real savages."

At the community gym today the girls all got together to come up with new ideas that would make our work out a little more interesting. They all put themselves in each other's power so that no one gave up. They did this for three minutes at a time by tying their legs together and as a group doing squats from one end of the 500 square foot room to the other end. If someone wanted to give up they couldn't; it was fun and also bonding at the same time. They did it to the count of ten back and forth. By the time their workout was done, so were they.

Yeti tells the girls she has a new workout that she wanted them to try next week for fitness fun. She called it "the rope." She says, "It is an exercise you guys will beg me never to show you again because you will want to die."

Doris looked like she just heard a dirty word and shouted, "No thanks, we have enough ropes around our necks. Let's skip that one."

Yeti heckled her and said, "One more will not kill you. Remember what does not kill you makes you stronger."

"You got my attention. You're on next week at 8:30 a.m. and bring enough rope for all of us!" shouted Flora.

The telephone was ringing when Flora got into the house; when she heard the voice on the end of the line she was shocked. It was her brother Alex.

The first thing he said to her was, "Just listen and what I tell you is to be put in a zip-lock," revealed Alex breathing heavy as if he had just ran a mile.

"I don't know if I can do that Alex. I never keep secrets from my husband especially if we can expect trouble out of this zip-lock worthy information," whispers Flora so that Dave doesn't catch on that trouble is on the phone.

"I am sorry sis I did not mean to put you in high stress mode. After all, we have not spoken to one another for two years now, and I call to drop a load on you. I did not do anything wrong in the normal definition of wrong. I am a victim of 'ears that have a mouth syndrome.' All that I can say is that a canary swallowed a worm that should not have been eaten. I cannot say anymore, you know the phone systems are infected with bugs. Can I just come and we can talk about it in person?" asked Alex.

"Well fine but if you get here and we think that you are headed for quicksand we are going to have to refuse to assist you and your baggage. Don't forget we are all just getting by and you will have to pull your own weight. Are you still cutting hair?" asked Flora.

"Yes, do you know anyone hiring?" inquired Alex.

"No, but we have much bigger plans for your skills. I will get the guest room ready. By the way, I miss you boy; I cannot wait to see you. Oh, how is mom? Is she still part of the informers club?" Flora chokes down the word 'mom' as she asked about her.

"There is a big reason that I have to leave this hornet's nest. I will leave today and I should be there around 12 p.m. tomorrow. I will travel light and use only cash so that I cannot be tracked. I have already destroyed the chip on my driver's license and I will not be using a regular cell phone. I am going to get a per-paid black market phone of course. I have a bud on the inside I will be cutting his hair before I leave. I know how well you and mom get along. I will not tell her what is going on. She is still part of the 'informers club,' so I am afraid of her as well," confessed Alex.

Flora and her mom's differences in ideologies caused them to become like 'seething foam' to one another. That was not always the case. They once shared a very close relationship. Her mom was like the tree that caught the plastic bag that went flying in the air without direction; she would catch Flora before things ever got too high over her head. Her mom gave her direction and inspired her to be a nurse just like herself.

Flora chose to take the side of "just because it was right." She has been the driving force in her community. Although her efforts at first were considered rebellious, in time with the opening of the cans of truth, she was no longer looked upon as a rebel. Thanks to Flora the community all works together and are much better off for it.

The door slams shut and in storms Dave. He and Mr. Deer had just returned from the home owners association meeting with the community planning board. She thought that it was safe to assume by the slamming of the front door that their appeals fell on deaf ears. She did not want to make Dave relive his voiceless door endeavor, so she just pretended not to see him while she continued to make dinner.

Dave came out of the room after about five minutes and asked Flora to forgive his rudeness. He then proceeded to vent "Do you know what happened or more like what did not happen?"

Not letting Flora reply back, he started rambling on about what he termed the, "swelled helmet heads." Dave continued with his rant and said "It's whatever the gunk face tarts want, we are at their mercies."

Flora did not want to start any new fires so she just listened as she rustled with the pots to find the right size top that fit the pot she was about to cook in. She seemed to be somewhere else as Dave talked. Although she could hear him, she was somewhere else.

Dave stopped his babel and said, "Why are you not throwing down insults as I replay my ordeal at the meeting? What is wrong with you? Are you sick or something? Where is my wife at?" Dave stands next to Flora as he holds her free hand and asks her what is wrong.

Her mind was lost in space as she was pondering what was to become of all that they had. She suddenly felt weak at the knees and tears started to swell up in her sharp now alarmed brown eyes that have just turned dull to life. Holding back the sounds of sadness, Flora took a deep breath and proceeded to cut the potatoes for her famous 'potatoes soup' that Dave enjoyed so much.

Flora dropped in the last potatoes and admitted for the first time in her life that she felt powerless.

"Yes, Dave I do bleed red, I feel so blue inside and for the first time in my life I have no counter to offer. Let me just take this all in and after dinner maybe something will jump out and hit my subconscious mind," said Flora.

After dinner we sat down to watch our favorite comedy show '30 Rock' when a news flash broke across the bottom of the screen of the television: "Reminder, tomorrow all zip codes ending In 47 will be mandatory for vaccinations."

"Oh no!" screamed Flora.

Dave is confused as to why she is acting so surprised since they have been going for the last two years to the happy internment resort.

"Dave I was not going to tell you till you were in a better mood, but my brother will be here tomorrow. He will stay with us for a while. I forgot about this time of the year, and he will be here when we are gone. He will have no idea what is happening. We will be gone for a whole week. That reminds me, I better call Karla and Laura at work and let them know it is that time so that they can cover my shifts next week," said Flora.

Dave, with his spoon in path to his mouth, drops it into the middle of his half eaten soup. Choking down his last gulp, Dave says, "That is great. Why did you not tell me when I walked in? I know that one thing is clear and that is fogs have many meanings. He is either in trouble or he finally broke free from your mom, either way we are going to be in deep murky waters. I love Alex but you had better tell me what is going on."

Flora stood up and put on her stone face and replied back, "I have no idea why he is coming and to honest I really don't care. He is my brother and I am here for him no matter what. If you don't like it you had better lump it. We will both find out what is up when we get back home. I don't want to discuss it any further we have other issues to start packing up now."

Dave knew she was under just as much or more stress than he was so he decided to let the subject go for now.

As day turned into night Flora could not sleep. She was not looking forward to the next week and she did not know what to expect in the detection center. She was told so many different stories she did not know who or what to believe anymore.

The morning started just as Flora thought that it would. Everyone was scared and nervous about the unknowns that they were going to be thrown into before long. Flora and Dave take a moment to give each other some much needed support they both needed from each other. Jonas comes out of the room with his back pack full of things keep him entertained at the center. His parents gently informed him that he will not need anything in his bag because he will not be allowed to have it where they were going. Jonas makes a face of utter disappointment as he turns down his bottom lip and wrinkles his nose as he drops his bag to the floor.

The sound of noisy tires are outside of our window so we distinguish it must be our ride. We prepared our mental state and headed out to meet the rest of the clique.

## THE UNWANTED VACATION

The whole community are all rounded up and put in the 'wellness bus.' Every year it is understood that their community is labeled as, 'antiseptic wipes.'

They are called that because they always refuse to be vaccinated with tomorrow's cancers and brain disorders that will get them in the near future. They consider this operation 'wipe ups,' that door to door intimidation was not enough to break our will. This place is going to be so quiet for a week. Alex is going to think that he just stepped into an episode of the twilight universe.

Mr. Deer is exempt because he is the head of the home owner's association. He always makes sure that all of their pets are feed and walked. Alex can assist him with the tasks at hand; it will give him something to do.

We got to our destination and were shocked by the signs that were on the entrance. The signs used to say 'Work Program' in bright green letters. The new sign holder consisted of two trees holding a logo that read: 'Give us back our planet.'

The two tree sign holder was an especially nice touch. Flora thought, "What was that? We never took it. I must admit it was a clever way to make us feel guilty for not falling for the 'dirt worship.'"

Flora smiled not a smile of oh! How happy we are going to be, but a smile of we are in for a deep brain washing while we are here.

"Never let a crisis goes to waste," was a very popular proverb by our overlords these days. The only problem with that is that they purposely caused the crisis's that set fires everywhere.

In the past they were able to stay together as a family but this time things are different. They are now being separated by sex. Dave and Jonas are going to be together and for the first time Flora is going to be without them. They had to leave all of their belongings with the guards so that they could go through it all before they were allowed to have their belongings back. They were not going to be down hearted they were warned about these new conditions by the Larson's; they just conveniently forgot.

As they separate Jonas starts to cry and refuses to let go of Flora's hand. Flora bends down next to Jonas and holds him tighter than she have ever held him before.

Flora reminds Jonas that mama is always going to be alright, the one that really needs him right now is daddy. Dad needs his little helper. "Think of this time away from mama as a vacation from my mouth," Flora says choking back her tears.

Flora quickly gathers composure and lets out a yell, "You are always telling me to give you and dad a break. Well, today is your day so stop crying my little ninja. We will go back to where we left off this time next week."

Jonas cracks a half smile and whispers to his mom," don't worry mom I will make sure dad feels like you are here by moving all of his things so that he can feel like you are still nearby playing hide and seek with his things."

The rooms are much smaller, and instead of doors they have bars. There are three cots to a room. There is one set of bunk beds and the other is a single cot to the left side of the room. Flora is the third wheel in the room but the other two are super nice to her. There are cameras with microphones in each cell so that you have no privacy at all. She feels like even her thoughts are being summoned to silence. One of her roommates asks her what she is in for. Flora starts to laugh at the jail bird lingo that was about to take place. She points to her arm and she starts to laugh.

It does not matter to Flora. She feels no threat of them nor them of her. Flora had to use the bathroom before she even got situated into the room. She excused herself to use the little hole in the floor called the 'squatty potty' that was located just behind the partial wall at the back of the cell.

When she came out Flora shook the water off of her freshly washed hands and introduced her, "My name is Flora, and I am here today for not being a good little girl when I refused to take the mandatory flu shot."

Flora excused herself one more time so she could address the camera in the room, "I know you guys can hear me. Can you tell the maid that we need toilet paper?" screamed Flora into the microphone as she held up the empty roll that was in her hand.

"Jenny. My name is Jenny, but you can call me Jen for short. You have courage talking to them that way. I guess you are new to this," Jenny speculates.

"No, we were here last year but I guess they figured by keeping us together we were getting a free vacation. But the joke was on them. I really did need some space from the old ball and chain and my son could use a pause as well, so it is all good," jokes Flora.

Jenny proceeds to confess that the reason she was there was for identity theft. She had taken credit card information from her position at the bank and used it to furnish her home. She was caught not even a month later. She tells them that she had one year left but it was not so bad here; she has met nothing but good people while inside. She insisted on giving Flora the does and don't list so Flora could avoid the correction booth.

The other roommate joins in the conversation and says, "Just call me Pat, short for Patty, and I am with you on that shot thing. My aunt died from that darn shot. She didn't even have the flu. I took my shot this year but I am starting to worry about it now that I see so many people choose to come here over the pinch. I know you did not ask, but I am here for writing bad checks. I have one more month left on my sentence. I agree with Jenny. There are better people in here than out in the free world. Let's just say I will not throw out the baby with the bathwater when I get out of here. I have made some really good friends in here."

The next morning the 'Hammer alert' wakes everyone up with a heavy thumping that blasted out of the speakers throughout the center. They better be up and ready to work at 6 a.m. If not they will get hammered by the guards and miss out on a yummy breakfast which consists of a dry piece of toast, an orange slice, and a glass of water. We worked in rows of 10 to a line back to back. The blisters and cuts to our hands from the box cuts made this trip a real stinger. Flora's thoughts are with Dave and Jonas. She hopes that they are doing better than she is. Alex must have gotten to the house by now. Flora hopes he has gotten in okay. She knows Mr. Deer will make him feel welcome.

Dave and all of the men are working on the assembly lines putting together the new toys for the army. There are seven wars going on around the world. What a shame. If you heard the news you would think that it was peace. They're keeping peace around the world through what is called the "peace packs of wars." Internment members dare not say anything about this new way of peace or they could never get out of there.

One thing was for certain, we were not going to be enjoying our week apart from one another. Flora missed them so much and it was only ten hours since she saw them last.

## THE KINGDOM HUMMERS

Flora remembered Caroline informed her that she should find a kingdom hummer and befriend them. She raved about the songs that they hum were not only relaxing but very spiritual. Caroline said they were a weird kind of normal but that was better than normal and miserable. What does Flora care about spiritual? She does not have a spiritual bone in her whole body. Well, today she finds one. Her name is Clara and her humming is as soothing as the chirping of the birds from Flora's back yard.

One day the hummer stopped her humming and Flora joked and asked, "Hey, who turned off the radio?"

Clara smiled back at Flora and replied, "I was just about to change the tune what would you like to hear?"

"Excuse me," said Flora.

"That was a test to see if you were one of us," winked Clara.
"Well, I am not! So if you don't mind can you put on another tune that you think I would like and so far I love all of your hums," remarks Flora.

"Since you seem to enjoy my humming so much maybe we can have lunch together so we can enjoy some real life saving food together," whispered Clara trying to appeal to Flora's need for spiritual food.

Flora thought to herself, "Why did I not keep my big fat mouth shut? How am I going to shake off that tail? I really like the humming, but I don't want her beating the Bible drums on me."

Flora responded to the hummer, "No thank you, I will pass. I heard about you people from a friend of mine; anyway I don't care much for God because if he existed we would not be in the fix we are all in and that includes you. I don't know how you can be here so long. From what I hear you guys have at least six months service here for door knocking an annoying message about 'God's love.' I am glad I live in a gated community; it keeps people like you out. I did get a letter from one of you about two years ago. I was wondering how in the world you got our name and address. We are unlisted."

Clara cleared her singing lungs and responded, "Did you read the letter?"

"Yes, as a matter of fact I did and I thought it was a bunch of mind control stuff. It came with a little pamphlet that said 'paradise on earth will it ever be.' I read it but since I never owned one of those books called 'the bible' I could not or did not care to know what it said. I am too busy trying to fight off this new world order. I cannot worry about some fantasy. Anyway, the way I see it, God has not done anything to make things better for us. Although, I would like to know why does God have all of those fantastic angels in heaven for? They are probably just fanning him all day. Why if we had as many angels on earth as we do demons we might have a fighting chance," Flora finished her rant and continued to stack boxes.

Clara supposed in defense of the angels, "Well, I hope they are catering to God all day. We sure are not, but did you ever stop to think that maybe an angel might have put us together? You should think about it. They are working very hard assisting God in finding those with a heart for God. That is a lot of work with much responsibility."

Clara then asked Flora a question that would burn a hole in her conscious.

Clara asked, "You know 'Alice of wonderland,' if you ever really want to get out of the trap that the queen of hearts set for you, by your following the NWO into their rabbit hole. I challenge you to find out what the king of hearts has up his sleeve for the new world order . He might even have a way for you to get out of wonderland."

"Hey you two stop yapping and keep packing," screeched out one of the armed guards.

They both looked at him and the gun hanging loosely in his hand and decided to wrap it up. Although, Flora did not want to admit it, she had been cleverly smacked down by Clara's question. She fabricated a plan in her mind to apologize to her when she sees her again. She wanted to get Clara "back in the ring" and re-engage in reference to her trick question that sucker punched her and left her without wind in her pipes all day and night.

At the end of the work day members were all invited to attend a mandatory movie of their overlord's choice. They all looked forward to this part of the day. If you consider watching a fly lay its larvae I guess you would contemplate the compulsory movie a highlight of the day. They were being forced to ingest the new terms and conditions of building a more united planet. They were fed garage about how Mother Nature was here since the beginning of time and how they needed to be good little larvae and let mother fly teach them how to exist.

"I cannot wait for the day that the fly gets caught in the spiders web that it is about to fly into," thought Clara.

The next day Clara saw Flora and bumped her in the back by hitting her hip. She expressed to Flora that she was happy to see her again. Flora looked at Clara and silently said to herself that she really wanted to get to know Clara. Flora than told Clara that she will take her up on her offer. Flora communicated to Clara that she had five days left make her a believer.

Clara whispered, "Only God can do that but I will be happy to help water the seed."

Flora rolled her eyes and said, "Oh, boy! What did I just sign up for? I guess I have just been put on notice."

Clara and Flora made arrangements to start nourishing on that food the next lunch day.

Around 3:30 p.m. there was an announcement muffled by the sound of sirens blowing out everyone's ear drums. A scruffy voice announced of an attempted break out and everyone was going to have to thank him for the lack of dinner that night. Flora did not get mad. She respected his moxy—a term used by an old Italian friend when he spoke to Flora about her outspokenness. Unfortunately, no one else shared Flora's sentiments. The silence turned to loud screams of protest that were quickly squashed by the water cannons that drowned out their revolt.

The next day during lunch Clara walked past Flora with her lunch tray in hand. She gestured with her head for Flora to follow her.

Flora got up and sat down next to Clara and questioned, "What was that about?"

Clara informed Flora, "You were sitting next to a bug. What I mean by that was that the woman that was sitting next to you was an informer. She was really a guard that dresses in population clothing to hear what people are saying. The goal is to mix the guards in with the population so that they can listen to what is being said at lunch to see if someone is caught speaking against the hospitality or anything that is considered hate speech. That was their way of extending your stay. Remember I have been here a time or two. I know all of those wolves no matter what their clothing."

Flora replied, "Thank God I got a live one on my side."

Clara smiled and said, "Why Miss Flora you are already learning."

Flora smirked and said, "Get over yourself girl that was just a manor of speech but whatever makes you happy. Let's cut to the chase. I have three questions and if you answer them to my satisfaction I will continue to talk to you about this here God. The first question is why does he allow wickedness? The second is where are the dead? My father committed suicide and I want to know if he is in hell. And last but not least, I want to know what God is going to do to make all of this craziness go away? You have a lot of explaining to do Clara so now it is your turn."

Clara's response was swift as she addressed the first question with a question asking Flora, "Do you have children?"

Flora's answer was an even rapider, "Yes a son."

Clara says, "I like to teach people the way our Lord Jesus Christ taught. He taught in illustrations, so therefore, I will try and answer all of your questions with something that I think that you can identify with. Since you have a son I will use the illustration of a kid at your son's school to try to bring home the answer to your first question as to why God allows wickedness to go on. Now how would you feel if a kid in your son's school told your child that his mom (I am talking about you) is a big fat selfish liar and that you are keeping all of the best things in life for yourself? What if that kid goes on to say that you give him restrictions to control him? The kid than tells your child that he can take control of his own life if he opposes your will over him. He spikes the drink so to speak, by asking him, was it really so that your parents will punish you for going against their rules? Now your son is probably thinking it would be nice to stay up late, eat whatever he wants, play xbox and watch questionable moves till all hours of the night. Well, now it looks like your son got hooked by the bait of independence. Your son comes home from school and decides that the kid has a point. He looks at the cars and all the things you prohibit him from and decides to go for it. So one night he makes up his mind while you and your husband are sleeping, to take the car and empty out your bank accounts. He is going to get a head start in life by taking all that you and your husband worked so hard for. When you get up the next morning your car and money have been taken. He knew that you were going to be upset. He was going to hide from you until he realized that he still needs the security that you and your husband provide for him. Would you stand your ground and punish him, or would you allow him to subvert your authority over you? What would you do?" requested Clara.

"Well since my son is only six years old he cannot do much and I doubt that any kid in his school would have such an advanced mind at their age. Besides he is too small to reach the pedals," smirked Flora.

Clara responded with another question, "Let's just say your son is no longer a child of six but is 18. Now what would you do? The shoe is on the other foot now start wearing them."

Flora tilted her head to one side as she pinched her lips together while moving her jaw side to side as she mauled over this new scenario.

Flora stops and rebels by proclaiming, "Really you would do that to me? Well, now that you put it that way, I would have no choice but to find him and when I did find him, I will take back my car and kiss my money good-bye. I would have to put him in jail because if I let him get away with it once he will surely do it again. I guess he would be upset with me but since he was a first time offender he would probably get house arrest or probation. I would let him come back home but he would have to live under much stricter rules, and things would defiantly be different between us. I would not stop loving him but I have to stand my ground. Especially if I have other children that are watching how I handle the situation," commented Flora.

Clara claps her hands and says, "Congratulations, you have just stepped into God's shoes and I am sure it doesn't feel good," remarked Clara.

"That was kind of what happened in the Garden of Eden. Adam and Eve took it upon themselves to take what belonged to God because they wanted to be free of his control and be like him having all that he had. They wanted what they could not have and got what they deserved; which was a hard life without his hard work to back them," Clara continued.

"They had to toil and make it on their own. God did not turn his back on them. He did give them what they needed to survive. Just as you said that you would do, was just what God did. He did make a way out for the rest of his children through his heavenly son. But that was another story that I will use to answer your third question. We have to go now; the horns are blowing, but before we go I am going to ask you to consider divorcing your criticism about God since the solution you chose for your son was not so far off from his. I will answer your third question tomorrow," replied Clara.

Flora questioned Clara about the order of her questions, "what about the answer to my second question. It seems odd that you would skip that one.

Clara remarks," I need more time to answer your second question about the dead. I am going to have to be very careful on how I approach that subject and since I only get one shot at a slam dunk I need to make it my last response. Besides I am sure you would want to find out what is going to happen to all of the vultures that are circling our corpuses.

After work Flora continued to think about the logic that Clara was trying to teach her in her illustration. Clara did have a valid point and Flora was now on the road to understanding why God has allowed man to endure their mistakes. Nevertheless, she still felt an uneasy feeling because wickedness was allowed to go unchallenged for such a long time. She was hopeful that Clara was going to be able to help her understand why humans have to pay for Adam and Eve's sins. After all that kid in the illustration did not have to suffer any other consequences or so it seemed so to Flora.

Back in her cell Flora noticed that Jenny had a tattoo of the name 'Jesus' on her back. She asked her if she was a Christian and her answer shocked her. Jenny said that her father was a Minister of a church at one time. She said she lost her faith when her father was arrested for stealing over $100,000 dollars from the church's bank account. Jenny could not understand how he could t condemn her for having a tattoo of Jesus's name on her back when he stole from the very institution he said was from God. He turned her off to religion because of his hypocrisy which led to her lack of faith.

Flora was a little disappointed by that story. She wasn't sure if she wanted Clara to go on to their next study point. She thought that Clara would just minimize the actions of corrupt religious leaders and she did not want to give her that chance.

The next day at lunch Flora chose not to sit next to Clara. Clara thought it was strange for Flora to act in such a manner.

Clara got up and sat down next to Flora. She asked her what was wrong. Flora told her the story about Jenny's father. Clara made no excuse for his behavior. She then asked Flora how she would feel if she was accused of being a bad mother because another lady that lived down the street from her beat her child and she did not do anything to help.

Flora looked at Clara like she was missing a few screws in her head and said, "What does that lady hitting her child have to do with me as a parent? And if it would make you feel better, if I ever experienced something like that first-hand I would protect the child and call the police if I thought that that parent was out of control.

Clara goes on to inquire, "So based on your response you would not want to be judged as a good or bad parent based on what someone else is doing down the street from you. Whether or not you know what was going on, you have no control over other people. Likewise, you cannot and should not judge other Christians based on what someone else does. Please don't turn God away based on what other imperfect people do. We are all going to fall short but we get back up again, and again, and again. I would like to continue answering your questions if that is okay with you."

Flora felt consoled about her reservations and allowed Clara to go on.

Clara said, "I am going to say a silent prayer as I dive into part two of your 1st question of why God allows wickedness."

After Clara said her silent prayer, she continued with her explanation.

Clara informs Flora that she was going to tie in the first study with this study. She also reminded her to remember how she answered her question about how she would handle the situation with her son that wanted to be free of her control.

Flora readjusted her thinking to serious mode so that she could take in this very important information that was going to make a huge difference for her. She let Clara know that she was ready to go on and Clara went on.

Clara started with, "I am going back to the garden when our first human parents were left to do things on their own for disobeying God; well, and they were not the only ones that were outside of God's good side. Eve was deceived by a snake named Satan—the devil—and he was equally responsible for the reason man fell from grace with God. You see, he was a very powerful angel in heaven that envied Gods position as ruler over Heaven and Earth. He set out to get mankind to worship him instead of God. Satan deceived Eve by asking her a simple question. He asked her if it was really so that they would die if they ate from God's tree of the knowledge of good and bad. He went on to say that they would not die but that they would be like God knowing right from wrong. Just like the example of the kid at your son's school; which side they were they going to be on, both angels and humans would have to decide. We can choose to follow Satan's seed and his way of self-rule or we can line up with God and his heavenly son Jesus Christ whom is the seed that will provide for the humble ones of mankind. God knows that his adversary is not going to stop especially since the issue had already been presented of who's rule was better, Gods or Satan's. So therefore, he had to let it play out until he was ready to settle the matter and end it all. So it is really very simple, you can choose to worship God, or you can worship the devil. God has allowed man to experiment with every form of government so that they cannot say that he did not give them a chance to make things work. Have they been able to bring us happiness? Well, as you can see and history will further prove man cannot rule themselves apart from God. How is God's seed going to fix things? Well, I will need a lot more time to answer your remaining two questions and you are leaving tomorrow so give me your address and I will see you when I get out of here which will be in about a month from now."

Flora wrote her address on a napkin and gave her a good-bye hug. She thanked her for helping her understand at least one of her inquiries. Flora now understood why God allows wickedness. It became clear to Flora that everyone has a choice to make; you are either for him or against him. She put herself in God's shoes and thought to herself that she would have done the same thing, especially when there was so much at stake. Flora cannot wait to find out how and when God plans on taking over with his form of ruler ship.

Flora is to be with her family today that is all that she can think about. Flora is gathering her belongings when she hears the call for her sector of release's to go to section 19 in transportation. Flora passes Clara in the outside breeze way. Clara was on her way to the Union Room for daily exercises before work.

Flora whispers to her, "I will see you in a month."

Flora catches sight of her husband and Jonas as they walk out of the north gate. Flora waits for them so they can sit together. Jonas looks tired and Dave seemed depressed.

When Dave looks up and sees his wife's face his emotional state switches to encouraged.

Jonas leaps out of his sleep and into is moms arms as he screams, "Mommy buttered toast never looked so good to me!"

"Wow! What a nice thing to say to your toaster," said Flora as she smiled and gave him a rub on the top of his head.

"You know what I mean mom. You know how much I love toasted bread and you are the whipped butter to my toast. That is all I was trying to say. Dad and I had a rough time I don't really want to talk about it. I hope we never have to come here again. As a matter of fact mom, dad and I have decided to take the shots next year. We will take our chances with the side effects," whispered Jonas as he sat down.

Dave must have had a horrible time. It is evident in his lack of communication. All he wants is for Flora to hold him and that is what she does.

Flora is not so traumatized; she had Clara to comfort her. She feels super guilty that she is not as upside down as the rest of her clan. She just stays quiet the whole ride home. Her shoulder becomes a pillow for her husband and her lap becomes a cushion for her son. It is nice to be needed is all she meditates.

## REALITY BITES

Alex's big, brown; puppy dog eyes carried a smile as wide as the opening of the front door as he opens the door. They all grab at him as if he was a piece of cotton candy.

Alex stands up from the table and announces, "I have never been so happy to be anywhere in the world before. I did not realize how much I missed you guys until I got here.

He starts to tell them about his ordeal when Dave shuts down his confession and says, "We can talk later son we have tender ears around us. We will take a walk and discuss your living arrangements while we walk."

"Anyone wants some home cooked food?" yelled Flora as she scavenges through the fridge to see what was there.

"I will take anything that is not made with peanut butter or jelly," laughs Dave.

Alex jokes and says," You don't have to worry about eating that I finished it off yesterday."

Jonas snuggles up to his long lost uncle and kisses his peach fuzz face, as he suggest he should use one of his dads razors to clean up the gruff off of his skin because it made him itch.

Mr. Deer was making his rounds to welcome all them back. They see a strange van following him. Right away they started to feel 'sunk in sick' to their stomachs. They thought that he had finally turned against them. The van that was following him was nothing more than what he called the 'welcome wagon'. Ben filled the van with gifts of food that were distributed by his son. What a relief, their appetites are once again ready to devoir the mouth-watering cheesecake.

After dinner they went for that walk that Dave was talking about earlier. Jonas stayed home watching a movie and they left.

Dave started the conversation, "Alright Alex, give it to us the way it really is."

Alex stumbles over the start of his information as he utters, "I was told by a very official client of mine named Essam, whom is now deceased. Essam told me some very crazy info. He was killed the next day. Essam's death was broadcasted on the news as an electrical short in the wiring of his house. That house was new and he was in charge of all home inspections in our county. I knew Essam would have never over looked a wiring problem. He was the best at what he did and did not miss a beat. He was a good man I will miss him. He told me that things were not what they seemed and that he was in charge of new operations that bothered his conscious. He had to tell someone it was eating him up inside. I was the only person he told. He had just been given his new orders when he came for a haircut. I was informed that as of next month all parts of our region will be forced to give up their homes. He was one of the few top inspectors that knew this, and he felt like he could not go through with it. He was going to quit before he had to start the ball rolling. Well, he did not have to quit, in a sense he was fired. I feel like I have to warn people about this. Everything was in place and ready for implementation. Essam was going to have to fine homeowners a flat fee of 25,000 dollars for having any kind of water on their property. That was just one thing he mentioned. There was so much more. Such as, if your dog droppings are not picked up they will all be charged. The neighborhood residents will enjoy a 1,000 dollar fine regardless if they have a dog or not. He explained that the plan was to get everyone fighting with one another so that they could start fires community after community. It gets better. Just listen to this, Essam was especially heated up when they told him that he was to take drugs that were confiscated by local drug dealers and plant it in the houses that legal gun owners lived in. He had a list of registered gun owners and he was going to have to set them up. The goal was to take away their guns because legally a convicted felon cannot own a weapon. The overlords had not been successful at violating their rights. The dictum was there was more than one way to shed a gun. So many crazy things are going to happen. I have to get this information out. Will you help me Flora? You know that this was a global agenda so what do ya say? Are you in?"

Alex's anxiety level was rising to the point of concern. He had so much apprehension they thought he was going to explode. He was literally a walking time bomb. Boy, were they glad that he was able to let it all out with them.

Dave puts his hand on Alex's shoulder and asks him to take a deep breath and let it out slowly. He was trying to keep Alex from collapsing.

Than he asks Alex, "Do you feel better? Don't worry about getting out this information Alex. The way things are going it will not be long before all Hades breaks out. No one is going to be surprised; some people will fight back and others will go along to get along."

As they are walking Dave stops and picks up a rock the size of a toddler.

Alex and Flora looked at Dave with confused expressions on their faces; they both wonder what this is about.

Just then Dave says something that blows them away. "Don't worry about me this rock was going to be used in a demonstration for you guys; so please pay close attention. You both just see a huge rock but at one time this rock was a part of a much larger rock that has lost part of its mass before it got to this size; as time passed this rock had been chipped away from its original size and integrity."

Dave takes the rock and throws it down and says, "You see now it is broken into more pieces. This rock was a good example of what is happening to us. We are losing pieces of our original structure that was once rock solid. Just like that rock things are going to continue to chip away until we are left with nothing more than a pebble of what we used to be. We cannot change things. You are going to be safe with us son."

Flora shakes her head side to side as she claps her hands in approval over Dave's display of wisdom.

Flora hugs Dave and proudly says, "For the first time ever I have nothing to say. I am really impressed."

Dave holds Flora's face up with one hand and says, "I am a chip off of your rock. You are the glue that keeps us together."

Flora leans back in his arms and says, "You're my rock and I am the pebble. Speaking of rocks, let's go in and watch 30 Rock. Tina is going to her high school reunion. I don't want to miss this episode, it is one of my favorite and I could really use a good laugh right now.

The telephone was ringing as they enter the house. It was Flora's mother on the phone.

Flora takes the phone out of Dave's hand and says, "How did you get this number, what do you want?"

Dawn, Flora's Mom, replies in an irritated voice, "Well 'hell-oh' to you too, where's your brother? I know that he was there. I put two and two together and got you, besides he forgot that redial was still active on telephones. He has been gone for over a week and I have been losing my mind."

Dawn's voice was now starting to break up into a muffled sound of tears as she continues, "You were the last number he called before he left my house. Please before you hang up the phone on me let me say what I called to say. I messed up with you and I am sorry for that. I do love my children and Alex was my pride and joy. I don't know what was going on and I don't want to know either. I know what happened to his friend it was all over the news. I can only image that my son was a victim of a 'mouth that has ears.' I am not even using the house phone to call you. I have already been contacted by the officials and I told them nothing and I want to keep it that way. All I have to say was now that the 'ring toss' was in my corner I want to throw it back. I am not going to cash in my son for any amount of money. I guess you can say that I am no longer going to be turning tables on anyone anymore."

She chokes back her tears and asks Flora in a soft humble tone of love and care as she made a final request, "Baby girl, please take care of my baby boy; blood really is thicker than water and I love you both more than you will ever know. We have always been like two rams dodging at each other but as of today I am removing my horns and I mean that in many ways."

Flora cannot help but to turn into a leaky faucet of emotions. As she chokes back her tears she says, "Thank you mom, you don't know how long I have wanted to hear you say that. We will take care of him and mom please call back whenever you like."

Alex put his ears up to the phone to hear his mother's voice and softly murmurs, "I love you mom."

The steam rolling information that Alex shared with them did not really faze them. They were already slapped with a small dose of that reality just recently.

Reality had already bitten them all at home. They had already experienced many similar injustices all around the world. They all just sat back in their transcendent existence.

Flora's day off brought in a fresh breeze so she decided to sit on the front porch with Alex and indulge in some fresh home-made lemonade. They notice a car they do not recognize in the neighborhood. It was a pretty old and beat up. She was afraid of what kind of grounded up beef would be coming out. Just as her thoughts raced about the red jalopy car, it stops in front of her house. Low and behold, her eyes must be playing tricks on her. It was Clara. Flora jumps out of her rocking chair and ran to greet Clara. Flora screams so loud Alex covers his ears.

"I prayed that you would come and see me when you got out but I did not hear from you. I thought that I was going to be left behind as an afterthought. After all, you have been out for at least a two months now, expressed Flora.

Clara reaches into her purse and says, "This is why I did not come sooner."

She shows Flora a newspaper clipping written in Russian. She began to translate what it said in English, "Today we have mopped up a sect of want-to-be Christians that continue to preach under ban. The religious irritants amounted to 15. Their bodies are to be left outside of the village hanging on stakes for three days so that any others that are still around can finally get the message. The animals will feed on what the vultures don't leave behind."

Clara's hands were shaking so much she can hardly read the next line. Flora gently put her arms around Clara as she took the paper out of Clara's trembling hand.

Flora holds her and speaks, "I don't know what power was strong enough to keep you up right now but I am so happy that you are here with me. I want to comfort you in your grief but I don't know where or how to start."

Clara gently pulls away from Flora's embrace as she takes the newspaper clipping back into her hand.

# A World Of Change

Clara declared, "Let me finish please, I am fine now. The third one to the left of this picture was my mother. My brother was the last on the right. My dear brothers paid for me to go and bury what was left of them. It was a close knit town of people 200 villagers, and they did what they could to try and preserve as much of the remains as they could. I was told by a good friend of my mom that they died with courage and integrity. They did not try to escape or beg for their lives. She told me that before my mother was shot she called out my name. I will see them again. Remember your second question to me at the internment camp about where are the dead? Well, today I am going to give you the comfort that you and I both need."

Flora felt inspired by her strength. She stops and asks for forgiveness for not presenting her brother.

Alex gets up out of the rocking chair and walks up to Clara with his hand held out as he states, "nice to meet you, my name is Alex. I am sorry I did not get up when you got out of the car, but to be honest I am still shocked by what you just read. I was drawn to tears and I don't even know you. Please let us help you."

Clara says, "Let's help each other and by the way it was nice to finally meet you. Your sister spoke kindly of you in 'the joint,' And may I add you have a lovely smile. I know that should be your line, but I really mean it."

Alex turns tomato red as he smiled while he looked away so that Clara will not catch the red tones in his embarrassed flesh.

"Oh my, I think I made you blush," smiled Clara.

They all enter inside to relax when Dave comes out of the room still in his Star Wars Pj's.

Clara heckles Dave about his pajamas and he runs back to the room.

Flora goes inside and explains who their guest was. He changes his clothing as he laughed at himself. Clara apologized for laughter; she goes on to say that his Pj's brought her back to better days. Clara's brother was a huge Stare Wars fan. Clara takes a moment to ask him where in the world he found those threads.

Dave goes on to say that he was an avid shopper of the local goodwill, "I have to enjoy them while I can. I never know when things are going to be sold on ZBay."

Clara stops and looks at a picture that was on the French table between the two sofas as she inquired who the couple in the picture are.

Flora takes the opportunity to tell her it was a picture of their friends the Larson's. She went on to say that they were in the center where she was at about a year ago but they are home now.

Clara asks Flora, "Is this the lady that you made reference to at the center? I remember you told me that a friend of yours told you to look out for us. Well, I do recall her she was very sweet to me. We spoke a couple times in the center but we were kept apart because we were on different work details. I would like to formally meet her one day."

Flora signals for everyone in the room to sit down for some coffee and Cuban toast.

Clara starts the conversation with, "I come equipped with your answers about the dead. Does anyone want to be excused from this subject? If you do I will not mind. It is a very sensitive subject for me and Clara. I am here to help Flora understand where her father, my mother and brother really are."

There were no objections so Clara proceeded. As a matter of fact, their ears perk up with keen interest.

"Death has touched all of us," replied Alex.

Flora asks Clara if she has a bible. Clara tells them that it is in her mind, and that she does not want to take a chance by carrying it around. She assures them everything she was about to say was credible.

Clara asked if she could say a prayer. She wanted to ask God for his holy spirit to be with them so that she could use his power to teach them the truth found in his word the bible.

After Clara ends the prayer she shares a scripture found at 2 timothy 3:14-16 as she quotes," You, however, continue in the things that you learned and were persuaded to believe,+ knowing from whom you learned them [15] and that from infancy+ you have known the holy writings,+ which are able to make you wise for salvation through faith in Christ Jesus.+ [16] All Scripture is inspired of God+ and beneficial for teaching,+ for reproving, for setting things straight,* for disciplining in righteousness

Clara starts out by asking what they all think about the theory of hell. Alex jumps right in and tells her that he thinks it was a way to keep the religious leaders in control of the masses. He goes on to say that if there was such a place most religious leaders would be assured a space there. They are responsible for half of the child molestation cases around the world, not to mention that the other half is homosexuals. They stand up in their pulpits every Sunday and decree it was a sin, but they go out on Monday and hire a gay escort service to keep it on the down low. Those white washed graves are buried up to their eyeballs in crimes against humanity as well. He further relates an experience of a former client of his that was in Africa serving under NATO. He explains that his client witnessed the execution of 200 defenseless woman and children that were brought to a so called religious sanctuary. They were paid 1,000 dollars to bring the people there but when they got to the church their hell was just about to start. Those poor people thought that they were safe. Not more than half an hour later he could hear the rounds of machine gun fire mowing down the screaming and dying voices.

He told Alex that their silence was worse than their screams because he knew that they were all dead. He did not know that he brought those poor souls there to see their last minutes on earth; if he had known that was going to happen he would have let them go in the jungle. Alex's client told him that if there is a hell those maggots are going there. So like Alex stressed earlier, it was a ruse to keep people in fear so that people will pay for their life of luxury.

Clara agrees with Alex and says, "You are right on Alex. It is a way to control people. The Bible says that God would never let anyone pass through the fire. He actually punished his chosen people of the Old Testament for being guilty of passing their children through fire. He also said that the dead are conscious of nothing. So how can someone be in a fiery hell and be conscious of neither pain nor thought? Logic is all you need to understand. My last but not least example is that God tells us in the book of Revelation that the wicked are going to be destroyed and that their names are not found in the 'Book of Life'. So this Book of Life means to live. Our loved ones will live when he resurrects the dead during the 1,000 year reign of Jesus Christ; God has no 'Book of the dead' and eternal burning. If your name is not found in God's Book of Life you are not going to be brought back to life. So the short answer is the dead are just sleeping in their graves waiting to be woken up. My family and your father will be coming back during the resurrection spoken of in Acts 24 of the bible. Only God can judge your father. Just because he committed suicide does not exclude him from the resurrection. Don't forget when someone commits suicide they are most likely not right in their mind. God reads the heart not the intention."

Flora bangs her hands on the table and yells, "Those two-faced back stabbing pieces of garbage have put me through hell making me worry about my father and now I know the truth. I am free! That is the reason why I don't go to church because I feel something is wrong with people that say God is love on with one side of their mouth, and with the other side of their pie hole they say he is going to flame broil you forever. I thank you Clara and Alex. Alex your story really opened my eyes about the two-faced jackals. I don't know about you guys but I am going to go with Clara to her underground meetings to find real hope. There is one condition though."

"What is that?" asks Clara.

"That you people don't pass one of those money offering plates around," replies Flora.

"That is not a problem we have never, and will never do that. A very wise man named Jesus said, "You get free, give free," said Clara.

"Then I am there," whoops Flora.

"Are you guys with me," inquired Flora.

She stands up in front of the table like she is ready to go right there and then.

Alex and Dave are not as gung-ho as Flora but they agree to go as well. They waste no time in getting to those meetings and they all look forward to learning more from the Bible.

A week later they are awoken by the sounds of marching feet on the streets that morning. Are they having a parade so early in the morning and in this neighborhood?

Alex gets up first to see what the ruckus is about. He pulls open the blinds from the window and yells, "Ah! I don't think we are going to like this parade if you know what I mean!"

"What?" yells Dave?

"Get our backpacks on it is time to go. It has begun," yells Dave.

Just as Alex is about to close the curtain he sees Mr. Deer being dragged out of his house and led into the street by a pimple faced, over grown, boy scout looking boy not much older than Mr. Deer's grandson who is 17.

Mr. Deer screams, "Please don't do this we are a peaceful community. Why are you doing this? For God sakes stop this insanity!"

Alex wants to go out and help him but his efforts would be futile. He wants to look away but he feels like he is a magnet that is stuck in the negative side of his force.

The young thug decides to make an example of Mr. Deer's questioned resistance so he shoots him in the head. Alex is no longer stuck to the window. He drops the blinds and runs to the back door.

Dave and Jonas are right behind him but Flora has the bright idea of calling the 911 operator for help.

Flora is stunned by the outgoing message. It is an automated recorded message that says, "You have reached a number that is no longer in service or available. You are now under mandatory martial law evacuation orders. If you are a home owner you are to surrender your homes to the local resource authorities. Please don't attempt to run or resist you will be shot. You are to stay in your home with your door open to show you are not a hostel. You are to wait for transportation to take you to your new living facility. If you have any medical needs that restrict your ability to work you are to call #311 the ambulatory services. You will be picked up and placed in a medical disposal center near you."

Flora yells out, "Stop! Please stop! Come back they will kill you! It is over we are done they are here to make sure we get on the bus to where hell really is! And that is our new homes. The quicksand is now in full sink mode we no longer have anything to hold on to! Put your backpacks down! Let's pray for wisdom and peace we are going to need it!"

Alex opens the door to show them we will not resist. They hear gunshots coming from the Sanita's house.

They know Richie was not going to go without a fight. They hear him boiling over with fury as he yells out, "here is your lead filled sleeping pill. I hope you choke on it!"

The shooting lasts about 45 seconds and when the bullets stop flying Richie and seven of the invaders lay dead on his manicured lawn. His wife tries to hold him one last time but they subdue her and make her go inside. Flora hears Monica and the children crying. She wants to go over and console them but Dave advises her against it. Dave comments that Richie always reminded his family that he was not going without a fight. They will see him again in the resurrection. Monica was very strong in her faith. God will sustain her. They will all be together in the camp and surely they will get to minister to her when they get there. They all know that the only option left to them was to wait on the one up above to save them from the times they were about to endure.

"Get ready to load up and roll out," clamors a scratchy voice over the blow horn.

He further goes on to say, "Leave your house and car keys on the table. All gold and silver are to be put in a bag outside your doors. We will start loading up at 12 o'clock noon."

Alex was upset and tells his family that he was not okay with all of this and that he would rather fight as Richie did. He paces the room back and forth wearing out the rug for over fifteen minutes. When he stops it is time for them to get on the bus. They do not know if they are going to be together; but they hoped that they will be in the same area. Regardless, it is time to go. They took their last look around their home, took a deep breath, and walked out the door heads up and hands locked. Now they are going to see just how dangerous it truly was going to be.

# THREE EVENTS AWAY

"Welcome to the rest of your life," that was the slogan displayed on the gates of the new housing complex.

"I doubt that we will be getting much rest," whispered Flora.

They all size up the twenty story community or maybe it should be called a compound. It has barbed wire all around to make sure they all got plenty of rest—not!

Past, present, or future, the events that are engulfing everyone's present life circumstance are in fact issues of the past that have come back up to bite them in the behind of the future.

"The more things change the more they stay the same," are words that come with a bite that stings right about now.

They get off of the bus that tracked in 130 of them. At least they are together was what was going through their minds. Sooner or later the price of the supply and demand eventually forced down the cost of a society's collective worth. So this was the price paid by humanity for its social progress; minus the unfortunate fixed conviction of people who got what was coming to them. They were all about to get what they were worth, and worth whatever they got.

The grass roots that society thought they were trampling on actually used them as the dirt to firmly plant its true roots of their self-seeking values that led them there. The world runs itself; the people had only to leave it alone. The world turns was what they have come to understand. Humanities only hope was that it will turn a lot faster than it had up until now. It was what it was, so when humanity got lemons the plebs was forced to swallow the pits.

Flora looks at her husband and says, "We are going to rediscover our love for one another in a way that is going to be uglier than the day is long."

Although her sarcasm is expected it is not being welcomed by Dave at that moment. After all they are about to be dovetailed into a world that is like a scene in a movie that took place in other parts of the world. Those who have all the money are now in control of the ones who have not. The poor have nothing left to take.

Flora hoped her skills as a nurse will earn them a premium upgrade of their living accommodation over the common laborer. After all, prices are still calculated by the total amount of your effectiveness or so she hoped.

The middle class has been taxed into extinction only two classes existed. You were either poor living off of the divine will of your over-lords, or you were the over-lord. This human power did not result in human happiness. The thought that the fire pan was better than the fire was truly flawed. What we did not realize was that either way you got burnt. Everyone wanted their piece of the American pie at the expense of the rich. They wanted a fresher version of the new deal but what they got was a raw deal. Never pay for the same real estate twice; another good principle to live by, but our society paid for it twice over by our poor choices.

# A World Of Change

Our civilization assumed that they could have their cake and eat it to. Well, cake never tasted so hard and bitter than the slice served. The light of our own candle was burning in someone else's wick. Humanity was considered to be human resources or in other words sources to be used by 'repugnant humans.' Our light houses were in stormy waters and in contrast to where their ships were supposed to take them. Being born to die was looking more and more like the shifted ill's that are about to plaque them all. For over 50 years life expectancy had increased from that of 50 to 60 years to well over 100 with the advancement of artificial arteries that keep tickers running and hips in place. All of that progress was about to take a deep run south of the border. The healthcare system that was now in effect worldwide was going to see to it. Everyone clamored to have the inequality of healthcare restored to a level that everyone would prosper and live long. They were wrong, It was only going to benefit the healthy and the strong but buyer beware if you were weak and fable you're sure to see the end of a cold steel table. The Powers, of the powers be, were sharpen by the mastery of time. History always repeated itself, especially when it was always meant to be used as a blue-print to be refined. The pure and endless darkness of time turned from minutes, to hours, to days, into years of an altered expanse of relentless powers that surpassed ones of old. All of our society's wealth and toys made our culture poor in spirit and weak in mind.

The country was divided into 10 zones run by 10 governors. The agenda for the 21$^{st}$ century took away all private property and gave it back to nature so that the earth could be transformed into workable areas with a controlled amount of people not to exceed one billion people on earth. The perfect storm of chaos hit us all. Humanity tried to weave and bob it for as long as they could but in the end they all got sucker punched into a 250 square ft. room. When they walked in they were greeted by a scantly furnished room that was divided by a half wall, which separated you from a room that contained three twin size cots one for each of them. The blankets were an interwoven burlap material that felt more like straw. The kitchen was equipped with just enough essentials for the three of them. The table was attached to the wall so that it could be folded up and down to save space so that they were given enough space to do their dally exercises at the 6:30 a.m. roll call. They were given 4 sets of state issued clothing to be washed by hand. They felt like they just went back 100 years in time. They could have at least given them a wash board. Outside the window was a clothing line for them to hang dry their hand washed clothing.

"So this was what socialized living looks like," snarled Flora.

Dave stopped and gave Flora the look of, "I am not in the mood," as he stood firm and just starred her down and let her have it. He returns fire by saying," this is your way of dealing but as for me and Jonas well.....we need some time to take it all in before you start your fill-a-buster of trash on us."

Flora looked as if she wanted to pass gas, held in the hot air she wanted to let it out on her husband. Flora decided it would be in her best interest to keep peace; after all he was right and she was wrong.

Flora changed her tone and said, "So this was what harmonized living looks like; there, I re-framed my sarcasm to something you can swallow without making me want to throw up. Ya, I guess we can forget that warm papa John's thin and crispy pizza that we so often craved. I can dream, so shut it."

Jonas snuggled up into my arms and said, "It's alright mommy we are going to be closer than we ever imagined."

Flora locked heads with Jonas and said," if I ever needed a life jacket it was now and the sea of my life has now come into view in your eyes my son. I must admit I am happy be the uterus that you came out of."

"Sick mom but I would not expect less from you," laughed Jonas.

"Do you think we are part of a video game?" asked Jonas.

"What you mean son," replied Flora.

"What I meant was that maybe we can level up if we are good with the weapons we are given," replied Jonas.

"Nice analogy son, I guess we shall see," sighed Flora.

The walls have ears and eyes, so they were careful not to say anything that would give away the notion that the zombies in room #180 were not sucked dry by their reality TV programming. Their pension for eating flesh was flavored with a symbolic vile of salt that was injected into their daily diet of propaganda. Just when they started to settle into their, 'when ignored all is good' mind set. They were called from their wall monitor doubled as a television that turned on at will.

All of the sudden the face of a condescending woman took over their mood with an announcement of their new names. "Number 606 that were Dave's assigned 'number name' take your tools and report to sector #12 to your position in metal works. Number 607, Floras new-fangled name; to sector #15 you will be working in the regeneration tissue lab. Last but not least was, Jonas number 608 he was ordered to report to SKY-1 for his higher learning program.

. "NYC" was labeled all over the compound. No! It did not mean New York City. The initials stood for 'Never You Care.' Those acronyms were there to remind them to mind their own business with their eyes wide shut.

Flora prayed that the shame and indignity that they were about to endure would leave them quickly. She was tempted to deface the sign by drawing a stick man figure with his finger pointing up. It was a nice thought while it lasted. Flora had to be careful not to smile too much or someone would have the impression that her thoughts were up to no good, and that would have been true.

The wheels of industry has been virtually stopped leaving them to just basic needs. The plus side was they no longer had to worry about 'keeping up with the Jones'. Flora did not have to worry about paying 10% of her meager paycheck to buy Jonas a new video game for his Xbox 360. She no longer needed to worry about sacrificing for that Victoria secrets bra that did not give away that she was a "B" cup while it lifted her to a 'C'. Aw, the blessings in disguise are really starting to look good. You have to find the bright side of the dark to keep from the blow back that stress can wreak on your body.

"CHECK POINT AHEAD" read the sign as they entered their work areas.

They were mocked by the sodium fluoride mind control freaks that had free reign to further degrade their self-esteem on a daily basis.

"Empty your pockets," yelled out the boil face adolescent looking man that gave us our daily shake down.

He made sure that they completely turned out their pockets from the inside hanging out like a tongue. Flora did not want to give them the satisfaction of barking out their medieval-ism reminding her how powerless she was. So she always displayed the tongues before she even got to the check in and out station every day. Flora smiled as she walked into the microwave ovens that were sure to seal her body with cancer. You can say that it would be an answer to her prayer of making her stay here as short as possible.

A loud dull siren sounded at 12:45 p.m. every day to let them know it was time for their portion controlled meal. Flora Looked forward to this 30 minutes of me time. Walking up the stairs She sees Clara. They gave each other a mind hug, as they stretched open our eye's to show their excitement for seeing one another again. They grabbed their lunch and sat next to each other. Clara started to hum a kingdom Song.

Flora asked Clara, "Can we take our lunch breaks together so you can share more stories from your spiritual mind? I enjoyed what I have learned so far and I want you to continue teaching me all that you know. "

"We can," replied Clara.

"I have it all in my memory banks it all flows back into my soul like tasty sugar cookies that will fill the very walls of my being just thinking about them. You know Flora I prayed that we would find one another in here. You are an answer to prayer for me," said Clara in a genuine happy voice.

"I too said a prayer but I am afraid mine was not so upbeat. I know you are going to soften the blow for me," answered Flora.

"What section are you working in Clara," inquired Flora.

"I am working in the assembly line that assembles the tell-a-visions," replied Clara.

"Gotcha! Watching TV was never a past time for me. I could not stand all of the reality TV shows that just drove me crazy," spewed Flora.

"How do you like being a movie star in this reality show?" asked Clara, as she inspected the peanut butter and jelly sandwich she was about to choke down.

"Well it would be better if I was getting paid, but I am learning to be cleverly dumb, you know what I mean," bellowed Flora.

"I am afraid I am not that talented but I get it," countered Clara.

As they said their see ya's, they re-framed from showing emotion so that they could not be used against each other in the future. Tomorrow was going to be another day that was sure to bring them face to face with more garlic knot morons that will try to dip her in their red sauce.

"How was your sky training son," inquired Dave.

"Well dad it was interesting. I felt like a chicken egg that was being sat on by a duck. We are treated exceedingly well for eggs."
"Eggs," added Dave.

Jonas proceeded to elaborate what he was taught, "The class is being taught that we will have to hatch out of our old way of thinking and we will evolve into a superior being that will rival our parents; is what we are being told. We are learning about the theory of the 'herd instinct.' Our mentor, that's what she called herself dad, so take that boiled look off of your face. We were all informed of how important we are going to be in the furthering of our future, and the war against the terrorist ideals of freedom and religion, both ideologies have caused all of the problems that have put us in the terrible fix that we are in worldwide. We were all give a choice of a puppy, 'the gift of life' program is what it is called. We get to train our puppies two hours a day. Depending on how fast we can get them command trained we will be given higher status in the class room; I want to make class president. Dad they live great, they have lots of food and water with cozy little houses that make us look like the caged animals, "said Jonas.

"Ah! Let's keep this between us for now; mom will not be so calm about this," said Dave.

"You got it dad I have already resolved that in my little head that was why I am telling you, "said Jonas.

Be quiet the big bad wolf was coming I can hear the stomping of her clogs'. I need to warm up dinner for us, "said Dave.

"Not again," groaned Jonas.

"Yes, left over food from 2 days ago hot dogs and beans," replied Dave.

The door did not slam today as Flora walked in.

"Where is my wife," exclaimed Dave as he looked to make sure it was Flora that walked in.

"Why honey, I do think that I have rubbed off on you in positive way," smiled Flora.

She responds," I had a great day, I saw Clara today we sat down together for lunch. We will be meeting every day for what we call, story time. She has given me the inspiration to see that there was light at the end of this dark tunnel."

12:30 p.m. only fifteen minutes until lunch. Flora watched the turning of the constant ghost on the wall as their hands had 15 more rounds to go; it was worse than waiting for water to boil. Anticipation for today's story was all that was on her mind. The bells went off and so did Flora.

Clara, sat down and slipped Flora a wrinkled up napkin and said," I am going to finish where we left off before we got thrown into the joint, sort of speak. We are three events away, this napkin is going to remind you of today's story so hold on to it, you will need it afterward."

"I took it in my hand and thought to myself, boy did I meet my match, this girl was a serious nut job," thought Flora.

Clara opened up the napkin and placed 10 pieces of crackers in it and told me to eat them one at a time. As I was chewing she counted each one out until I finished all of them. In my head I thought, "This better be good."

Clara said, "You just ate all of the major parts of the ritual devotionals that were supposed to feed the world spiritually. The spiritual food that they produced left them spiritually empty, just like the crackers you just consumed that left you hungry for real food, when our world leaders are saying, "Peace and security" than sudden destruction will be instantly upon them, just as birth pangs of a pregnant woman it will be. This is a time for us to keep comforting and building up one another because things are going to go from bad to worse overnight, like a thief in the night. All of the sudden the mountains (world leaders) will restrain the stars (religious leaders) and put them in shackles and stripped them of their glitter and glory they will reduced them to dust. The sea (the people) suddenly had no direction to go, so the sea (people) was running here and there wildly hitting the sides of the mountains (governments) and drowning in the sands. The mountains will say to the stars, "Where are your leaders? Why don't you call out to your empty symbols and idols? Who will save you out of our hands? Why even your God has abandoned you into our hands. No money in the world can cover all of the blood that was spilled in all of your names. "The mountains took away all of the stars powers and locked them up in clouds of confusion; while the clouds were covering the stars the sea's agitation gave way to grief. There was a small puddle of water left in the sand that seems to know just where they were going. So they stayed still, quietly waiting to be swelled into a new stream of water that would safely take them out of the angry sea and the clashing mountains, "explains Clara.

Flora was left in the sand; sort of speak, as Clara ended the story for the day.

"The horns a blowing so keep the napkin to wipe up the drool off of you face," smiled Clara.

Flora was left holding her breath when she said, "gee that was nuts. The mountain, stars, and sea all have a new meaning to me. I have to remember that 'peace and security' was not what it supposed to be. It is going to be the beginning of the end.

The next evening there was a fire in sector #8; that put the community in total lock down. One of the numbered zombies used a torch to set a fire in the computer control room. He was quickly subdued and the fire put out. Everyone was shocked to see someone had enough courage to take on their task masters. Unfortunately, he was going to be made an example of what happens when you try to break out of their control grid.

We were all forced to watch the community news at 8:30 p.m. to witness his execution by a firing squad. Defiant to the end was this stout red haired Irish man with courage that made him sound 10 feet tall.

He was ordered to turn his face to the wall but he resisted and said, "I want to see it coming when the bullets relieve me of this useless existence."

Two men held up their guns in the firing position, the man lifts up his hands in the air and shouts," fight back whenever you can, show them that resistance has many levels," was the last thing he said as the bullets went flying.

They covered our eyes and said a silent prayer him and for his family. They were not going to be a party to that thinking, even though it seemed to be the honorable way to go. They were going to put their trust in a higher power.

After school Jonas took his puppy home as a treat today. He had lots of toys and a soft cushioned bed for it to sleep in. It was so nice Flora wanted to sleep in it.

"Mom, look I did so well today that mentor Jenny let me take Rexa home," said Jonas.

Flora bent down to pick up the black and white snoopy looking puppy when it just about took off her nose.

"Nice puppy what is it mixed with poison and fur!" shouted Flora.

"She is a rat terrier mom," said Jonas."

"Well I must say if the name fits you must permit," and I can surely see why they permit that bread to exist she is as mean as a switch on a thorny tree!" snapped Flora.

"She is nice to me mom, she only does that to protect me. I am her human and she is being trained to respond to protect only me. I feel like a king around her; she hangs on my very being. I will get an 'A' for parent detection training of Rexa. You see mom, there is a picture of you and dad on my desk and Rexa is wearing a video camera on her collar that is recording everything while we are home. Rexa is trained not to let you or dad near me. You cannot raise your voice over a certain wave length without triggering her to attack you. She has already passed with flying colors, because as soon as she saw you she tried to bite you," said Jonas.

Floras face grew five inches of furious. She knew that the tell-a-vision was watching her so she walked out of the 250 square ft. dungeon. She did not know how to react, but she knew that she had to, or she would explode inside of her tormented soul. Her brain was scanning options when she surrendered to a thought that calmed her down enough to go back into the room.

"Jonas darling, pictures can be used to bring out the good and bad in someone, why don't you put up a picture of all of us as a family. Let me take a picture of all of us so you can replace it with the one you have, than maybe she will not hate us," replied Flora.

"Well, mom I will have to ask Jenny if that would be allowed. I don't want to rattle her cage," replied Jonas as he lay on his cot rubbing Rexas' belly.

Dave tried to pick up Rexa when a hostile voice yelled out over her collar," Parents are forbidden to touch the animal so back away or you will be shocked!"

Dave hides inside a shell of disbelief; as he slowly backed away from the dog feeling as if he had just been castrated as a parent.

Flora took the napkin from lunch and gently wiped away the tears from his long drawn face of hopelessness. No words were spoken. Their body's language was weak and depressed. They both seemed to have lost the fight that they once thought they had. Their little boy was being used against them and they were powerless to do anything about it.

Flora was distracted at work the next day. She kept replaying all of the details of what happened with the dog. The timer on the tissue regeneration tube went off but Flora did not remove it on time. The tell-a-vision started to yell at her and called her insulting names.

She than gave her a wakeup call that could not be ignored as the voice from the tell-a-vision shouted," let that be your first and last mistake. If you burn another batch you will be terminated! You will not be going to lunch today. Pick up the mess and start all over again."

Flora knew she meant what she said. She has to stay alert; Flora cannot afford to take risk like that. Her family needs her to stay focus.

Flora said a silent prayer that went like this, "Please God give me peace and allow me to use all of this persecution as a way to grow closer to you. I am new to this and I don't know if I am saying the right words. I know that you read hearts so please read mine and let me know what is in It." Flora ended the prayer in Jesus name, amen.

Clara knew something was wrong when she did not see Flora at lunch. Knowing that it would be risky to leave her housing section was not an option. She had to check on Flora after work. Clara knew that unless you were a hall monitor you could not leave your sector. Clara had a neighbor on her floor that was a hall monitor, whom also enjoyed listening to her stories. Clara asked her friend if he could check on room 1806 to make sure Flora was alright. She gave him a copy of today's story written on one of her inspection sheets neatly folded up.

Flora and Dave heard the knock on the door and they both jumped out of fear of what, or who, could be behind that door. Dave opened the door and saw a tall muscular man dressed in blue and white attire.

It was a hall monitor, Dave took a deep breath and said, "Yes is there something wrong."

"No, sir can you step outside for a moment, "asked the mild mannered man.

Dave closed the door ever so slowly.

The tall man slowly leaned toward him and handed him the note, he then said, "Clara sent this have a good evening sir."

"Flora, it is a note from Clara," said Dave.

Flora Jumped up from her bed and began to read the letter to herself in the only spot of the room that she could not be seen from the tell-a-vision in the room.

The opening statement was a sincere hope that all was fine. Clara opened with we are now going into the second event.

This story is a little complicated so I will break down all of the symbolic meanings as I go. "We left off with the puddle of water in the sand. That puddle of water that was left in the sand stayed undisturbed, while the rest of the sea was being thrown about. All kinds of trouble were thrown at the sea (the people). Please pay close attention and focus on this next phase."

# THE FALL OF BABYLON THE GREAT REVELATION 17 EXPLAINED

Flora now shook her body as to say focus, girl focus. She took the letter and began to read the meaning of the symbolism of revelation 17.

Clara's letter started out with," the stars will be finished off by the mountains in this second event.

The harlot was devastated and made naked by the mountains. **The harlot represents religion and the mountains mean world leaders**, but how do we know that? Flora I want you to stop and take a moment to think about what does it mean to be a harlot?

Flora put the letter down and thought to herself, that a harlot was a prostitute or a promiscuous woman. She picked up the letter again and continues reading.

To help you further understand I am going to use an example of a married woman that claims to be loyal to her husband but she sold herself to other men to keep herself in a better financial position. Well, this is the way that God views the religious leaders whom claim to be married to him spiritually, but they sell their support to world leaders while they commit spiritual fornication with them. That is why they are called the harlot. As a matter of fact, they don't acknowledge Gods kingdom but support human governments as the answer to mankind's problems. They go as far as denying God his personal name and reduce him to the title of lord. There is something seriously wrong when the creator of the universe is not allowed to have his personal name known. He will avenge this insult and like he said in the book of Ezekiel "they will have to know that I am Jehovah."

Flora puts the letter down again and passed her left hand up and down past her face 3 times. It was her nervous tick and she was nervous. She wanted to stay focused because this was very important for her to fully comprehend. Flora took a breath and continued. Clara comes to life again as she resumes where she left off.

Now Flora I am going to explain to you the meaning of the names of the world powers that were foretold to be in control from the early bible times to now. The world powers are listed in their order of sequence from Bible times up to the present day world power. Be patient with yourself stop if you have to so that you can really digest where we are at in the stream of time, now let's go.

And there are seven kings: five have fallen- represents world powers that are no longer world powers in control of other nations: Egypt, Assyria, Babylon, Medico-Persia, and Greece. All of these world political powers held power before Jesus Christ became messiah.

The one that- is- represents Ancient Rome-the world power when John wrote the book of revelation. The other has not yet arrived. When John wrote the book of Revelation this seventh world power did not exist yet, but in our day it has arrived. This one is our current world power, but when he does arrive it must remain a short while. The world powers before lasted for long periods of time for example, Rome were the world power for over 1000 years. So therefore, the 7$^{th}$ world power, which is the last world power; will be in power for a short while in comparison to the other world powers. Now let's continue on.

Now let me help you understand the identity of the "wild beast," The best way I can help you understand is by giving you another crash course on just a few of the symbols used to represent countries that make up this wild beast. Let's start with Great Britain their symbol is the mighty lion, China is the fierce dragon, USA is the tenacious bald eagle, and Russia is the ferrous bear. Now when you put these symbols together you get a "wild beast" and what does a wild beast do? They kill and mangle need I say anymore. Now keep going.

And the "wild beast that was" (stands for the former League of Nations)but is not; they fell apart and got back together and changed their name to the 'United Nations.' It is also itself an eighth [king], but springs from the seventh world power "The Anglo American world power made up of the USA and Great Britain formed the League of Nations after World War 1; it is now the United Nations renamed after World War 2. The United States and Great Britain are the Anglo American World power that is the seventh world power prophesied to be the world power in control when God's kingdom takes over. No other world power will take their place. As a world power they are going down with this sinking ship.

Flora it is important that you understand the spiritual significance of the numbers in revelation we will start with the number 10. It is key to understanding the symbolism of revelation. Number 10 represents earthly completeness in connection to man. To help you understand I am going to give you some examples: we have 10 fingers and 10 toes, Moses gave 10 commandments, and finally the 10 plaques on Egypt. do you get the picture. The number 10 means the total number of, or complete amount of a group in relation to mankind. Revelation 17 and the number 10 is our next lesson.

"And the ten horns that you saw mean ten kings, who have not yet received a kingdom, but they do receive authority as kings one hour(here is the meaning of this). There are 190 countries that make up the body of the United Nations. They co-share authority over the world. They dictate global policies such as sanctions on countries that they feel do not meet the standards they set globally. They also control the world's monetary fund or in other words 'the money' through the 'IMF,' trade through the 'WTO', and the food through the 'FAO.' these are just a few of the organizations that they control. These smaller countries that make up the United Nations have the power of a king by being part of this global ruler ship." It is common knowledge that the United Nations are the ones that are currently taking over countries such as Greece, Italy, Cypress, Spain, and Portugal. These country's economies are being raped by the bailout funds that have been bank-rolled by the 'IMF'. The world economies including the United States and Great Britain are being exploded inside out from top to bottom. All of this is happening to give the United Nations ultimate power over every nation through these so called bailouts; which are more like take overs.

Flora had to stop again because now things have started to make so much sense. All of the pieces are now falling into place. Now she understands why the 'IMF' has control of all of the world economies and why the world trade organization is in control of all trade between nations. They control everything, and the book of revelation is right on I am ready to commence with the rest of revelation 17.

These have one thought, and so they give their power and authority to the wild beast. The waters that you saw, where the harlot (representing false religion) that is sitting on (many waters represents peoples) and crowds and nations and tongues. The ten horns that you saw and the wild beast, these will hate the harlot (false religion) and will make her devastated and naked (false religion) will be stripped of their wealth. Their lies and crimes will be exposed rendering them naked to the peoples that they have deceived to their end.

The beast will eat up her fleshy parts and will completely burn her with fire. Fire means permanent destruction. **For God put [it] into their hearts to carry out his thought, even to carry out [their] one thought.** So we see here that although they think they are in control of the take down of false religion it is actually God that is using them to bring about his sentence of death upon the ones that claimed to represent him and his son but as you can see he does not approve of their terms and conditions; so they will go out in the blaze of his wrath. Just as the bible foretold things are going forward until the words of God will have been accomplished. The prophet Daniel **at Daniel 2:44 said," in the days of those kings the God of the heavens will set up a kingdom that will not be brought to ruin. It itself will not be passed on to any other people, it will crush and put an end to all these kingdoms and it itself will stand forever."** We are now living in that time of the end of those kings. God has prepared his kingdom and is now ready to take over. He is using the current system of governments to do it. Just like he did with his chosen people of Israel when he used the wicked king of Babylon to take his people into captivity for all of the gross sins they committed against him. History repeats itself with Gods people on earth in our day. Christians are supposed to live their lives according to the standards that Jesus set. Soon very soon we will see who really followed his ways. We are coming to the end of this lesson. Flora stay with me I only a few more symbols to reveal; after all, the meaning of revelation means to reveal not to keep it a mystery; as so many people have claimed it to be... So to the final revealing of the last part of revelation 17 are next.

And the woman (Satin's seed of religion who is also known as the harlot) whom you saw means the great city-Babylon the Great the Empire of False Religion. Now I am going to give you the back ground of the original Babylon from the bible book of Genesis. The beginning of false religion and all of the pagan practices that originated with mother Babylon are still in full bloom today. When God saw what they were capable of building the tower of Babel in Babylon, he confused their language so that they would cease their agenda and spread out according to their language. When they did spread out they took with along them all of the Babylonian teachings and practices taught to them. This is the reason why it is called Babylon the Great. Its influence had flourished into a much greater version of its mother Babylon and, so therefore, it was called Babylon the Great. The apple did not fall far from the tree. All of the pagan celebrations and traditions still exist up to our current day. Babylon the Great yields great power and influence over many people and nations. So the complete destruction of false religion is the end game in the second event."

"I believe we are going to need to have hope out for faith, instead of hope for faith" thought Flora.

She came out of the room looking like she had just swallowed a knowledge pill. She pulled Dave into the bathroom and told him to read the letter and he will be just as enlightened as she was.

One hour later Dave came out scratching his head and said," well, it makes sense and I am happy to know that the stew that was cooking our goose has a meaning. The only problem I have with all of this is I that I don't know how to put faith in someone I know so little about; we are so new to this that I don't know if we are going to be strong enough."

Flora held Dave and said, "God reads hearts and intentions, I know your heart and your heart is good. We just need to pray to him and continue learning from Clara. The more we learn the deeper our faith will get. Remember what she said, "those calling on the name of Jehovah will be saved," Well, we are half way there; now all we need to do is build up our faith through prayer and our good friend Clara will help fill in our knowledge. Trust me, God will do the rest; we are taking in the steps in the right direction."

Dave was on his way to work when a hall monitor stopped him and asked him to go with him. Dave went but was not anticipating a good out-come. The man took him to the hall monitor that brought him the letter.

"Hi my name is Carl," he reaches out his hand with a warm smile and went on to say, "I read the letter that Clara sent you and I just wanted to let you know that I know how you must fell today. You see, I have been learning from her as well. I found it very hard to believe but after a few hours of thought I knew it was all true. We can help one another. I got your back man I just wanted to let you know that following darkness as a dream is not going to be our future." Carl and Dave shook hands and went their separate ways.

Dave thanked Carl and told him that he now knew that God was looking out for them and he was happy to have him on their side. Dave continued on to work when he left Carl. While there he could not escape talkative Joe who had a bad reputation of talking too much. Dave knew Joe was about to start his babel because his mouth was moving in his direction.

Joe says, "Collapse always comes at the beginning, rather than the end we were given the Colombian neck tie in 08. We were killed economically and were all left with our tongue's hanging out since then. So break the mirror in your mind, so you can see a friend from a foe; which are you friend or foe?"

Dave looked at Joe and said, "Which one are you?"

"Ah! A question answered with a question, that's fair," Joe replied.

"I am not so black, as I am painted; I do wear a white hat," smiled Joe.

Dave gave way to laughter and said, "a friend that is my answer, now let's get back to work Glen the "whip master" is looking this way. "

Lunch time today was going to be explosive like a volcano. This information was boiling over lava hot. Because not only did Flora understand the second story, she was now able to put times and events in its proper place and completely comprehend what was to come next. She was ready for the third and final event to be explained.

Clara walked in she did not seem to be quite herself today. She had tears in her eyes.

"Clara what happened," Flora in deep concern asked.

"One of my sisters has been killed this morning. She lived in my sector. Apparently she was caught telling one of our stories to an insider that turned her in for an upgrade in living standards. You will hear about it later this evening on the tell-a-vision. She was a pillar of strength to us all. They gave her a lethal injection and it was over in less than 30 seconds. I will see her and all of my loved ones again, and when I do they are going to come out their memorial tombs just as Lazarus did. I will see her and my family members that are alive and well in Gods 'book of life' that their names are written in. This dark cloud has a bright rainbow just around the bend," replied Clara.

Flora was afraid to ask about the third Event. She thought it would be in poor taste and that Clara needed some time to be alone in her grief.

Clara quickly brush the tears away from her crying nut brown eyes and said," are you ready for the third and final event."

Flora was pleasantly surprised to see that Clara still had the strength to tell her the last story. Clara than injected a shot of reality when she said," I have to tell you now I never know when I am going to be found out. I want you to know just in case I go away; you will have all that I had to give you to make this life worth pressing on for. Now let's go backs to our first story where that little puddle of water stayed waiting for a larger wave of water to take it safely out to sea. In the final days of all false religion; that little puddle of water that represents the true servants of God that are dwelling relative security, they are now going to undergo some turbulent waters before they are taken to security. Why were they being left alone for so long? They are part of a religious group are they not? Clara sparked Flora's interest when she intrigued her thoughts with those questions.

"Okay you have my attention," said Flora as her ears seemed to have perked up and grew an inch or so not to miss a word.

Clara continues, "The reason they were left alone was because they did not get all wrapped up in the political end fighting over the loss of their rights of freedom of religion or any other political matter; they stood completely out of the way, you know that old saying, 'out of sight out of mind'. They recognized the fulfillment of bible prophesies and know that by getting involved that they would be fighting God himself. It was God putting these religions on the cutting block to resolve his issues with them on the matter of how they treated him and his people. He wants them to know that he was the one coming after them for their blood guilt. Unfortunately, when they do realize what was happening they are going to try to make a last ditch effect to reason with his son and profess their loyalty to him. What is his son's answer going to be to them? I got your answer.

Jesus is going to say to them, as Matt 7:22-23 reads, "Many will say to me in that day, Lord, Lord, did we not prophesy in your name, and expel demons in your name and perform many powerful works in your name? and I will confess to them; I have never knew you get away from me you workers of lawlessness I never knew you," than he will drop his hammer on them. Never again will God or his son Jesus allow Gods Sovereignty to be put on the back burner, from Armageddon on God and only God will control all that goes on in heaven and earth. He will use his only begotten son to do all that he wants done. You see God is going to use one part of Satan's organization (or seed) to get rid of the other part of Satan's organization. In other words the wolves are going to turn on their own pack. They were always running in the same circles and involved in the same schemes against humanity. "The faithful followers of Christ are by no means getting away unscratched. No, they have the devil on their tails and he is going to be as a roaring lion. He is going to become unchained with anger because Jesus has used his own weapons against him and his time as ruler of this world is up. So now he is going to go after Gods people with a fury. He is going to try and make optimal impact on the poor little defenseless flies stuck to a paper sort of speak. It appears that they will become the object of an all-out assault by many peoples. God's Word describes that development as the attack by "Gog of the land of Magog, Ezekiel 38. How should we view that attack? Knowing in advance about this attack on God's people does not make us overly anxious. Don't get me wrong we have no idea what he is going to do to save his people out of the clutches of Satan's forces. All of the devils earthly and demonic forces are going to come in for the kill against Gods seed heavily and earthly. Satan and his demons are going to make war with Gods people on earth, as well as, his heavenly angelic forces lead by his son Jesus Christ. When Moses had his back against the wall at the Red Sea God showed his strength and power by delivering them out of the hands of the full strength of the advancing Egyptian army, leaving them at the bottom of the Red Sea. His loyal servants will be up against the wall as well. He will deliver them as he has done before but in a much greater scale. He will save those calling on his name. They will have to know that he is "Jehovah God Almighty" and he will defend his name, and his right to rule all at the same time.

In the mean time we kingdom hummers, that you so wisely nicknamed us, use every opportunity to strengthen our faith so that we will be able to keep our integrity to our God "Jehovah" no matter what hardships we may encounter and there will be many. Teaching you about God and his prophesy, not only builds my faith but it gives me the strength to go on. People like you, that are looking for answers and want hope for the real life that we have been deprived of is what stirs my tea," remarked Clara.

"What should I do?" asked Flora.

Clara responds, "don't worry that is the first thing you should do. Keep on the watch for first of these three events and pray for strength. Keep learning and most of all pay it forward by letting other people know about Gods kingdom that is just around the bend. What domino will have to fall to trigger this attack? We don't know but like I said before we need not worry about it. God will intervene. Zechariah 2:8 says, "He that is touching my people is like touching my eyeball." Your eyeball is the most sensitive part of your body; your eyes lids protect your eyeball almost instantly. Well, that is how sensitive God is going to be about his people and those whom want to harm them.

## The Third Event-The Attack of Gog

The next day Clara asked Flora to be even more attentive to the next lesson. She tells Flora that this next section is going to make more sense when they are actually in it the thick of the prophesy. Clara goes on to explain.

"The third and final event will climax into the battle of Armageddon. Regarding that war, God declares by means of Ezekiel found in Ezekiel 38:1-6 where it says, "'I will call forth against [Gog] throughout my entire mountainous region a sword, is the utterance of the Sovereign Lord Jehovah. Against his own brother the sword of each one will come to be. Panic-stricken, those on Satan's side will be thrown into confusion and will turn their weapons against their own ranks—soldier against soldier." However, havoc is also to come Satan's way as Ezekiel goes on to say: "Fire and sulphur I shall rain down upon [Gog] (means Satan) and upon his bands and upon the many peoples that will be with him. What will be the result of this divine action? God will use the rulers of this world and their own tools of cruelty and destruction against each other. The snake that started all of this trouble in the world will himself be shaken knowing that he is really done. The nations will have to admonish that their devastating defeat was brought about by the order of our God Jehovah himself." Clara ended her study and asked Flora to please recap what she just said so that she can know that Flora really understood.

Flora recaps what she understood and that was that the devil was going to come after Gods loyal followers. They are going to wind up on the other end of their own spears, sort of speak. They are going to turn their weapons on each other, and the devil will also meet his end at the same time. Clara pats Flora on her back and tells her that she was the sharp end of the pencil and she had nothing else left to teach her.

They wrapped up their study and went back to their jobs. They both left with a great sense of achievement. Flora felt enlightened and hopeful and Clara felt confident in knowing that she has given Flora all the knowledge she would need to jump start her faith. Clara gave Flora three very big injections but she knew that Flora could handle it.

At the end of Flora's work day she had a renewed sense of hope. She was hungry and was counting on a good meal to wash down the spiritual banquet she consumed earlier. As she walked down the hallway she sees a little girl drawing a picture outside of her apartment.

Flora decides to take a look at what the child is drawing. She bent down next to the child and said," I love art what are you drawing?"

The child look up with her sky blue eyes and said," tell me what you think it is and I will tell you if you are correct."

Flora paid extra special attention to the colors that the child used. Flora's smile was wiped off of her face and her continence became disturbed by what she was looking at. It was a hangman's noose hanging on a tree that was shaped like the salute of a woman. The sun was red and blue with little parts of the sun falling off in the color of blue size balls. The ground was covered in what looked like piles of the leather hides of dead animals. Flora had no idea what was going on in the child's mind but at this point she just assumed to forget asking the obvious. She wipes the smile off of her face and gets back up off of her knees. Flora back up slowly with her hands clinched and her head shaking side to side in disbelief.

The little girl asked her, "don't you want to guess, are you not interested anymore?"

Flora started to walk away when the child yelled out," that is my mother in a form of a tree. The rope represents the hang man's meat hooks, and the floor is covered in the skins of all the animals that have died because of all you meat eaters. You all must be converted into mother earths subjects or the sun will die and so will we."

Flora rumbling in her stomach has just turned to knots. When is she going to wake up? What is becoming of their innocent children? Who is in control, are the kids going to be the end of them? Flora caught sight of her apartment and ran a little faster; she than remembered that she had her own chicken little at home. She wonders what surprise he will have for them today.

Dave was on the floor wrestling with Jonas and carrying on as if all was just fine in room 1806.

Flora smiled and jumped on top for them and said," I win let's eat.

"Dave made a cake for dessert and boy were they happy. Flora and Jonas had not seen one of those for at least 3 months.

After dinner Flora shared her experience about the little girl with her family.

Jonas reported that the little girl's name was Angie. He told them that everyone called her, 'the art tart'. She is always drawing twisted things that she says are important for them to take the lead in educating their parents.

The other day in school she drew a picture of her parents being walked on a lease by her dog. It was funny," said Jonas.

"Jonas please stays on our side. Please don't get sucked into this rabbit hole of power over your parents. You are supposed to listen to us. We know what is best for you," begged Flora.

"I know mom but we are being re-shaped into our new future and your old ways of thinking are going to have to go to sleep. If we are to have a life of real social change we have to start from the ground up and we are closer to the ground than you are," laughed Jonas.

Flora was feeling that perverse knot in her stomach again as she thought to herself, "Three events away."

## Peace And Security

It has been one week since the encounter with the little girl that Jonas called art tart. Everything seemed to be becoming more and more normal as the days turned into weeks. They were all getting used to the conditions and it did not seem so oppressive anymore. But that was the calm before the storm. Things were about to go south real soon. There was an announcement made earlier that day for the entire compound to go to the assembly hall by 7:30 p.m.

There was not an empty seat in the theater. The entire community compound was ordered to appear in the assembly hall. The movie screen came to life right at 7:30 p.m.

An Asian man whom stood about 5'3", wearing a red robe with a red hat that was shaped like a cross and sickle: addressed the world as the executioner of the divine will of universal power and authority over man and God. He then went on to direct everyone's attention to the screen that was covered by a long black curtain which was now slowly inching open for the unveiling of this sardonic event.

He started with showing live action footage of all the worlds' religious leaders being rounded up and taken into custody. He then said "You are witnessing for the first time in history the freedom from religion." As you can see from our live global satellites the world is simultaneously witnessing the cleanup and removed of the cancer you once called 'faith'. These faiths have deprived humanity of true "peace and security." No more wars will be fought in the name of the Cross and the Crescent or any other symbol. On screen you are seeing all religious temples, buildings and their assets being put now under our control. The global society will now have true peace and security without their unrighteous meddling."

After his presentation he did something that we never expected to see. In a gesture, as a challenge; he welcomed anyone in the audience to come up to the stage and chose a weapon to fight for their religious rights and leaders. As the lighter that was meant to spark a flame, it was on. The Global news teams were on site to record the clash for later prosperity.

"Our leaders have fallen," shouted a tall dark husky looking man, who became the match that lead the charge for the weapons on the stage. He was the first to grab a gun and as he held it in the air he shouted, "This war is for God."

Children that were in the audience start screaming and crying because they were afraid of all of the bawling and screaming that their outraged parents broke into. They paid no attention to logic and ran up to grab a weapon heading head first into the flames that were intentionally prepared for them.

"Come fast!" shouted Flora, as she yelled out for Carla and Alex to come and help her round up the children to safety.

Her plea for help was responded to by all the other unwilling participants of the religious revolt. It took only a matter of hours for the clash to begin and end. There were soldiers outside waiting for the armed zealots. They were dropping like pebbles hitting the ground. They hardly got off any rounds. Their plan was successful. When the dust from the bullets settled there were 15,000 men and woman dead or injured in our community compound alone. The number of people left in our compound was a mere 2,000. I admit I am not happy about the loss of life but I was happy to still be a subscriber of life.

That night there was footage posted from the slaughter worldwide. Our local officials were literally laughing while burning the bodies as soldiers used the tip of their automatic rifles to burn marshmallows over the physiques of the deceased.

They were singing an interesting tune that went like this, "down they fell one by one the harlot and her flock has all been done, so next in line, and let's has some more wine." They sang that song the whole time they were roasting their marshmallows and drinking wine.

The Global media covered the events with a fervor of extreme jubilation and pride that could only be matched by reaction to the fall of Germany after the Second World War II. There seemed to be a calm after that day that lasted for about one week than the second domino began to fall.

## THE ATTACK OF GOG OF MAYGOG

The cry of peace and security produced a quick and bloody skirmish, but their circumstances were about to take a drastic turn North. The latest incident occurred this morning after our morning exercises. We were told that as a reward the remaining labors were going to receive double the amount of work and they all knew what that meant. They were rubbing salt in the communities wounds.

Flora looked like she wanted to checkout as she asked Dave for his hand to help her get up off of the cot that had now felt like all of the springs just popped.

Dave wiped the sweat off of his face and replied, "Well I cannot say that I am surprised we did loose most of the workers but I figured they were going to be bringing more people in. I guess we will never see each other now.

Flora stood behind Dave and tenderly hugged him as she told him, "don't worry honey the days will go by so much faster and before you know it we will be in a new system of things with a government run by Jesus himself. We are only two events away and I don't know but I think these last two are going to be pretty soon. We have seen the call of 'Peace and Security' prophesy eludes that everything was going to happen very fast from that point on.

The very next morning brought in the next drop of bad news for their slave community. The tell-a-vision woke us up earlier than ever. It must have been about 3 a.m. in the morning when we were all told to get up and report to the community center for interrogation. The children were to be left in the rooms.

There we were all informed that this was going to be our working hours and that each of us will be questioned about their loyalty to the Governor. Anyone who does not sign the dutiful form will be dealt with.

Dave and Flora refused to sign so they were put on the list for operation wipe up.

For the next 24 hours the" youth brigades" made their way to each labors room to begin the inquisitorial of the children. They were putting on the lights; sort of speak, to extinguish the rest of the cockroach Christians that were smart enough not to be part of their first bon-fire. Their group overseer told Clara to get them a message through her floor monitor friend. He urged them as true Christians to avoid direct confrontation with the authorities and to direct them to him. He will make a stand for them no matter the cost. Don't let them use the children; stand firm and not let Satan use your children to compromise anyone. That is going to be their way of breaking your spirit. The youth brigade stated their rounds, starting from the southern side of the building. They did as the group overseer advised and it resulted in his arrest by the Security forces. His appearance was that of an esteemed middle aged fellow with the stature of humility and meekness. He clearly was not a treat to anyone.

Brother Combs addressed the Russian official that gave him a chance for a last-minute appeal but he kindly declined as he went on to say, "In what seemed to have become standard procedure in the elimination of Christians of your first purge, that tactic will not work with us. We have no intentions to resist with violence. We will not hold against you what you are about to do.

There is an avenger for us and he will hold your feet to the fire of his destruction. I may die at the end of my speech but I will live again not for the fight but for everlasting life without the threat of ever being harmed again by the likes of your kind. The venue will be the same minus you and your leader Satan the resister of God. There is no fear of you here. We are joyful about the events that are about to unfold. Our Gods performance will be a sold out event from one end of the earth to the other,"

When he finished the men looked at one another, as if they were saying, this man is out of his mind. The tall bald officer said to him, "the wind that just came out of your wind bag will be the last that will leave your pie-hole. I'll tell you what I am going to do. I am going to let one of your fellow believer's do the honor of killing you for me. He scanned the room fill of integrity keepers in search for the perfect trigger man.

His eyes fell upon a young man about 20 years old as he said, "Hey you there with the bottle cap glasses come and waste this piece of trash for me and I will spear you and your family. I will thicken the pot by making you the king in this community. What will it be man?

He started a count of three when the young man stopped him at two and said, "No need to go any farther if you want him dead do it yourself. I am with him and I will die with him. We are all of the same resolve so no matter who you pick in this room they are not going to do your dirty work."

The officer took his gun back from the young man and pointed it at him to see if he would beg and plea for his life, but he did not even blink an eye lid. The officer was crazy mad at this point as he stared to yell out obscenities, while he flung his gun around the room in frustration. He could not get a rise of fear out of them and that caused him to feel powerless, therefore, causing him to lose his mind."

"What is wrong with you re-fried beans. No one is going to save you today or tomorrow. Did you not see what happened to all of your religious leaders?" said the officer.

Flora cleared her throat and said," those were not our leaders; our leader is not of flesh and blood. Do with us what you want; there is nothing that you can do that he cannot un-due."

He lost it at that moment and just shot brother combs himself. No one showed emotion they just started to hum a kingdom melody called 'he will call.' The men left without the satisfaction of breaking their will. It is still uncertain, however, whether the rest of the assembly of God fearing people were going to meet the same fate, but compromising was defiantly off the table of options that they had availed themselves.

The use of the inducement of force was deplorable but they were already prepared for worst but hoped for the best. They were taken out of the assembly area to be dealt with by a force of their peers.

Dave held my hand ever so gently and without haste he whispered to me, "I have never been more proud of you for speaking up the way that you did."

Flora smiles her half-hearted smile at Dave and alleged, "Round two is coming up, I hope we can endure it without falling apart."

Dave replied, "Not even death will keep me from you. Up to the neck means up to the neck. The threat of death that was challenged once can be challenged many times over. It is the first test that makes the second on expected victory."

As they were lead out of the room they had another party waiting for them. The remaining people in the compound were waiting to take part in their own form of public humiliation.

Flora says to herself round two coming up. Their stabbing eyes made them feel like they were about to be put in the blades of an electric fan. One of the labors threw rotten eggs at them, while the others joined in with shoes, and rocks.

"No evil spirits to ward off here," said Flora. As they endured waves of vicious attacks each corridor that they passed.

"God help us," Thought Clara as she was started to feel week from the anxiety. Alex could see that she her legs were shaking and she might not make it. Alex used his strength to keep Carla from crashing to the blood drenched floor. We got to the outside of the commune where buses were there waiting to take the loyalist to God knows where. The waiting soldiers had their guns drawn pushing them onto the bus.

One of the Russian soldiers yells out to his boys in a menacing voice, "do you have the marshmallows we can take our time with this next batch of maggots!"

This was a time of atrocities, and there was no one to save them. They were not looking for the parting of the big yellow bus, but it would be nice right about now. They were on our way to the pits that were made for bulk killings.

Something in the road stopped the bus. No one did saw what it was that interrupted there joy ride, but no matter how much the driver hit the exhilarator the bus did not seem to budge.

Dave took the lead in a prayer as he asked, "father thank you for giving us the strength that has keep us going up to now. It must be you, because we have no will of our own anymore. If we should all perish at the hands of your adversary, we only ask that the world would soon see the sanctification of your great name and the restoration of your ruler ship. I pray this in Jesus dear name, AMEN."

They all opened their eyes and they could not believe what was happening before their eyes. The bus was floating in the air. The driver had a heart attack from all of the excitement. The steering wheel was moving as if someone or something was controlling it. It was then that everyone knew that they were in the hands of the angels and spirit sons of God were taking them to a place of safety.

"Thank you Jehovah," they all said in their loudest voices. They started to sing their favorite song, "We thank you Jehovah. "The collective consciousness all knew what was coming next.

The felling of dread had completely lifted off of everyone's hearts and minds. The manifest evil was now in a deeper level of trouble than they ever were. The bus was filled with the spirit of salvation and delivery. The joy of this moment in forever is now our forever.

## Armageddon

The bus that they were in, landed on an empty corn field. They looked outside of the windows to make sure that it was safe to come out.

Jonas screamed out, "hey you guy what is that thick black blanket that is covering the heavens."

The atmosphere was turning darker and darker by the second and before we could blink an eye we could no longer see anything at all. It was as if the light switch in the sky was put in the down position.

Alex walked to the front of the bus and announced, "I don't know about you but I think it will be safer inside than outside. Maybe whatever is going to happen will end quickly but I rather be here together as a group than out there being subjected to God's you know what! Exclaimed Alex."

"Amen," to that said the group in agreement.

Right after Alex stopped talking the lights went completely out from the heavens. We heard what sounded like the stampeding of hundreds of thousands of horses, but we could not see them. We could feel the vibrations coming from every inch of the earth. The sound was defiantly from the firmament. There was no doubt at this point that the battle of Armageddon was about to take off.

Just like a kernel of popcorn being pressurized in a popcorn machine the earth started to exert a great mass of force from the heavens to the bottom of earth's core, everything started to shake while the sounds of thunder and lightning rang out so load, we thought the windows to the bus were sure to shatter.

"Are you scared," asked Jonas to his mom.

"No, honey we are under Gods protection from this point on. Let's sit back and watch Jesus and his angels fight Satan's forces, both spirit and man, "said Flora.

They all sat back in their seats and pretended to have front row seats of Gods real 3D premier movie called, "Armageddon."

"So do you think that at this point everyone is still clueless as to who is behind all of this," asked Jonas.

"Well, if they don't it is because they want to live their last moments in denial, but that will not last long because look what is happening to the atmosphere now, "shrieked Flora.

The dark blanket that covered the sky now started to break apart into small flickering pieces of fire sparks that looked a lot like a firecracker sparkler when it is lit up. A thunderous voice cracked open the rest of thick black blanket as the sound of a giant zipper zipped across the expanse of the heavens.

The voice of ages announced," vengeance is mine, the one who is and will always. I am handing all of my enemies over to my son to do my bidding for me. All of those who proved my adversary Satan the devil a liar by sticking by my side and calling upon my name; stay still and watch your salvation. You all will now know that I am Jehovah and there is no other God."

The scepter and crown of Almighty God Jehovah was about to go into action with his son Jesus as executioner of his great war of Armageddon. The angels that were standing at the four corners of the earth holding back the winds of destruction were now given their orders to let go and assume their fighting positions.

"Now the popcorn is about to start popping," said Jonas.

Just then all of Gods natural elements came into full impact. Huge chunks of ice rock, fiery asteroids, disparaging comets, ferrous winds, caustic rains, and massive earthquakes that were so powerful they made the greatest structures on earth cave in like toy Legos, all of Gods forces went into full action wreaking havoc upon unrightous mankind. Just then relentless rains began to fall within a few minutes and as a repercussion, we had cloudburst and landslides. That was an unnatural disaster but the huge devastation reduced hotels and homes near the flood path into agate fixtures just floating passed our bus.

Dave took the dead bus drivers satellite cell phone to see if he could see the damage around other parts of the earth by using google earth. Some things you cannot un-see and this is what he saw in California. The effects the mega earthquakes were the strongest in the history of the world. The surface ground cracking associated with faults that reached the surface caused horizontal and vertical displacements for thousands of miles. Its vibrations lasted for hours causing mass wave amplitudes in unconsolidated surface material, such as poorly compacted fill or river deposits; bedrock areas receive greater effects. The worst damage occurs in densely populated urban areas where structures were not built to withstand intense shaking. There, L waves produced critical vibrations in buildings and break water and gas lines, starting uncontrollable fires. Damage and loss of life sustained during the massive earthquakes resulted from falling structures and flying glass and objects. Flexible structures built on bedrock were generally more resistant to earthquake damage than rigid structures built on loose soil but in this case everything was equally disturbed. In certain areas, the earthquake triggered mudslides, which slipped down mountain slopes and buried all of the habitations below. A submarine earthquake caused a tsunami. This series of damaging waves rippled outward from the earthquake epicenter and inundated all the coastal cities to the demise. Dave put in another geographic location of Florida. This hurricane was the deadliest ever.

Flora took the phone from Dave and said," Please don't look anymore it is not going to do you any good to see so much death and loss. Just be thankful to be alive and thank God for his protection."

The loss of life was so extensive that it brought tears to Dave's eyes. His thoughts jumped out of his mind into the ears of the audience that were curious as to what he had seen. The destruction is worse than anyone could have ever imagined. Dave was grappling with very strong emotions for people he don't know. Nothing could be hidden from God. All of the rich and powerful were out of their flushed out of their hiding places. The price-tag was not enough to keep them from Gods View. Just as the prophet Amos 9 said came to be. There was no hiding place safe for those seeking to escape Gods day of vengeance. The mountain, oceans and even the heavens were wiped clean.

No more living a lie within a lie. All truth was exposed. The righteous ones are now on their way to living a life of purpose.

The children of God kept falling and yet he kept healing their wounds. If it were not for the fact that Jesus died for us and did not fear man we would not of had a change for a real life. The climax of the Gods day of anger had yet to come to its full finish.

Jesus the arch angel Michael was saving the best for last and now was when the steam was really going to heat up. The seemed to be a regrouping as we began to see pockets of foggy steam surrounding in whole field in a yellow powder that smelled like rotten eggs. Normally, our lungs would have collapsed but we were not affected at all.

What was about to happen, I would say is going to be the most exciting of all.

## Wickedness A Thing Of The Past

The world was about to witness the dragon, Satan the devil and his legions of demons being taken away to tartarus. Tartarus is a place deep under the earth, where only Satan and his evil spawn will be housed for the next 1,000 years. The sound of heavy metal chains seemed to be approaching from every corner of the earth. The sound was as nerve wracking. It was one million times the rigorous of billions of finger nails scratching across an enormous chalkboard. It was so intense that we had to cover our ears; not because they would burst but because it was an unholy irritant. The clouds once again changed back to its original color of white. The vapors suddenly started to take the shape of the chains that everyone around the world could hear.

The chains now were tightening as the contents inside were being tied up into triple knots of evil. This happened for hours. There was an exchanging of words between the Satan and Jesus. No one understood what they were saying because it sounded like an ancient language, probably Hebrew the original language given to man before the tower of Babel incident.

Who said the devil never cried? Well, he did today. The whole world could hear his whining as he was being dragged like a 100,000,000 pound ship anchor racing to the endless bottom of the earth. When the chains stopped moving there was once again a calm that came over the whole of earth. We felt a cool gentle breeze break way; it had the sweet smell of honey that left my senses in want of some tea.

Satan's days are over for now, just as Revelation 20:1-6 said," And I saw an angel coming down out of heaven with the key of the abyss and a great chain in his hand.[2]And he seized the dragon, the original serpent, who is the Devil and Satan, and bound him for a thousand years.[3]And he hurled him into the abyss and shut [it] and sealed [it] over him, that he might not mislead the nations anymore until the thousand years were ended.[4]And I saw thrones, and there were those who sat down on them, and power of judging was given them. Yes, I saw the souls of those executed with the ax for the witness they bore to Jesus and for speaking about God, and those who had worshiped neither the wild beast nor its image and who had not received the mark upon their forehead and upon their hand. And they came to life and ruled as kings with the Christ for a thousand years.[5](The rest of the dead did not come to life until the thousand years were ended.) This is the first resurrection.[6]Happy and holy is anyone having part in the first resurrection; over these the second death has no authority, but they will be priests of God and of the Christ, and will rule as kings with him for the thousand years.

The scene has already changed just by that breeze. It was deceptive because the mass destruction that was left behind was overwhelming. The dead bodies were in every corner of the earth. There was no closing your eyes to the destruction.

Everyone was in a state of elation to have witnessed their salvation from Satan's goons and Gods protection during his day of wrath. They were not far from the compound that they had spent the last six months of their lives in. Jonas started to cry thinking about Rexa.

He started to walk with a drag in his step and said," I hope she did not suffer I really love that little mutt."

Flora stopped and knelled down next to her son and said," judgment was for people not for animals, Rexa might be alright. We will go back to the room and hopefully there is some place that she took cover in."

It took us about 2 hours to get back to the rubble of the compound. It was completely flattened and Jonas began to cry once more.

The air was thick with smoke and ash. There were gas fires and internal explosions erupting all over the place. It was not looking good for Rexa.

"Stop, listen! I think I hear her," yells Dave.

Jonas ran over to the sound of a yelping cry. Jonas called out for Rexa as he ran toward the direction of the cries. Rexa hears his voice and comes running out of from the rubble of rocks that she was hiding under.

Jonas had never been so happy to see her little cow face. He kisses her and she licks his face so hard and long that all of the dirt and dust was completely wash off.

Jonas tells Rexa," I am so glad to see you my friend." Jonas eyes swelled up with tears as he told Rexa," You're not just a dog you are my best friend."

The words at revelation 22:14 are now accomplished as they read the scripture out loud, "Happy are those who wash their robes, that the authority to go to the trees of life may be theirs and that they may gain entrance into the city by its gates."

There were millions of righteous people popping out of the rubble of destruction that the great tribulation brought in from all over the globe. Just as Revelation 7:14 said, "These are the ones that come out of the great tribulation, they have washed their robes and made them white in the blood of the lamb."

They had all survived and lived to see the changing of the guard, from man, to a mighty spirit called Jesus Christ. Jesus was now in full control of Gods creations from heaven to earth.

We were all helping one another with an infectious joy of the miracle of survival from the total destruction of those found at revelation 22:15,"Outside are the dogs and those who practice spirits 'and fornicators and the murders and the idolaters and everyone liking and carrying on a lie."

They knew that they were now in the mist of the real change, into a world that would bring them true peace and security under Christ rule in Heaven.

Cold wars, civil wars, world wars, boarder wars, all wars will not occur ever again. The repressed human rights and excessive environmental damage were now going to be reversed. Human trafficking, which is one of the most heinous crimes against humanity is now abolished. No more servitude to drug addiction or alcoholism. Taxes, loans, insurance payments, mortgage payments, car payments and all of the material things that keep civilizations in bondage are now eradicated.

Farmers, builders and cleaners are now going to be the professions that we all will be perusing with a feverous want. The only college education humans will be needed will be taught right in their own home. Our higher learning will be from God. We will build our homes and plant our own gardens without anyone telling us how and when we can do it. Complete freedom from all form of governments is now over.

After Six thousand years of human history the only people that survived the war of Armageddon were of a humble heart. All that was wicked are a thing of the past. The yoke of sin and death was now a thing of the past. We are now moving into a time period of perfection. The original purpose for man and earth was going to be restored, with Jesus Christ as our king in his 1,000 year millennial reign.

# GODS PROMISES FULFILLED

Now there is a new exhilaration for living. The world in change became a world of change; no longer ruled by man but by one that ruled by spirit. We now lived in the world of change from a once desired democracy that fell short of man expectations; to everything in the hands of a great spirit that will make everyone feel extraordinary under his rule. No more will man become 'more than himself' but instead 'everything to all'. Hope is no longer a feeling to be optimistic about, it is now the prophetic fulfillment of mans purposed happiness. Contentment is longer to be 'an expectation' but our reality.

Just as Psalms 37:29-31 said," the righteous themselves will possess the earth, and they will reside forever upon it. [30]The mouth of the righteous is the one that utters wisdom in an undertone, and his is the tongue that speaks justly. [31]The law of his God is in his heart; His steps will not wobble.

The once divided earth has now reconnected. The world now has 70% land and 30% water. The aquifers were fully operational and ready to restore all life giving plants, stunning colorful dancing flowers, sweet fruit and shading trees, and mouthwatering vegetation back to its once opulent abundance.

Earths restoration to its original purpose of paradise is difficult but just as God had promised it is being accomplished. We were all overwhelmed, the cleanup seems endless, but sure-enough this is a bonding time that our kind has never shared in the entire expanse of time. Money doesn't make the world go around anymore, this is free labor left behind from the righteous war.

The Cosmic junkyard lingering in the heavens above is currently being cleansed by what seems to be a giant vacuum cleaner in the heavens sucking up all of the space debris. We could hear the smashing of the metals, glass and plastic materials which made up the satellites and space stations; now being crushed and deposited into the black hole in the realm of our unpleasant past.

Flora had no use for her skills as a nurse due to the fact that the effects of imperfection are evolving us into healthier beings. Time is now turning the other direction for humanity, from days of old to years of young. Skin is now shedding off raisin wrinkles and turning back to the re-invigorated spender of radiant hues of smooth fair tons of white, tan, and brown complexions as soft and smooth as a baby's bottom. A much anticipated promise fulfilled.

Yesterday Dave severed an artery in his left arm while welding a bolt on the bridge. Flora was not there to see it but what Dave told her astounds Flora. He recreates the event of how is hand was healed by showing her his freshly healed wound on his left hand; he then took her hand and put it on his skin. When his wife touches his hand it felt like a freshly baked bun that just came out of the oven, warm and soft.

"Dave why is your hand so warm, were you in the sun after your wound got healed" inquired, Flora.

"Nope, it was crazy; after the torch accidentally slipped out of my hand and burnt a hole in my hand. I felt no pain and I saw no blood. I thought that maybe I was going into shock; the hole in my hand starting to bubble up like hot lava coming out of a volcano. I could see that my skin was intensely hot but I did not feel any pain. When the bubbles went away my skin started to flatten and soften just like a snake peels off its skin; my skin peeled off the old tissue and grew new flesh right before my eyes," said Dave.

"That's not fair I don't think that I will ever experience anything that majestic, "gleams Flora as she marvels at Dave's newly healed hand that she continues to rub in her moment of amazement.

So many new people are coming into their lives and not one of them was the sort that brought with them the fires of persecution and crime. True peace and security "is here. There is a swiftness of the saturation of love for one another blowing in the wind. We are finally free from the atmosphere of inequality to equality that even an optimist would be surprised. Another wonderful promise found at Isaiah 2:4 is fulfilled that says, "and he will certainly render judgment among the nations and set matters straight respecting many peoples, and they will have to beat their swords into plowshares and their spears into shears. Nation will not lift up sword against nation neither will they learn war anymore."

A week into this new world, everyone was anxiously awaiting the opening of the new scrolls of laws that are going to be read to the global society. They expect these new laws to be the shattering of all the paradoxes of the past; to ones of the highest edification of mankind. Dave stood next to Flora while his fingers unconsciously stroke her hand.

They heard what sounds like the rustling of chairs coming from the heavens. Everyone is settling in for the immense experience that we were collectively going to encounter. The world was a grip in anticipation. The emancipation from the slavery that humanity was once bound to is for sure appreciated. Everything that humans could expect is now going to be "set in stone. "Thus the laws can be gleamed from one end of the expanse to the other. Gigantic stone walls were erected in their proper historical geographical positions around the world.

These series are made of stone, brick, tamper-earth, wood, and other materials. Each was placed there by the angels themselves.

Humility has nothing fear with reference to being criticized this day. Even "humble" attitudes can be masks of pride but not with our heavenly righteous ruler. Humility, is the freedom from one's self which enables one to be in positions in which you have neither recognition nor importance, neither power nor visibility, and even experience deprivation, and yet have joy and delight. Although, Jesus is our mighty king he has the spirit of humility, and that is the kind of leader we have in Jesus. He came to earth to live and die as a man so that he can be a just ruler that can truly understand where we came from and where we are going under his loving rule.

The expanse of the heavens opened up with vibrant colors of yellow, red, green, blue and purple rainbow clouds that shoot across the expanse of the sky as a warm voice descends from the clouds.

Jesus addresses his sheep like ones and says. "Welcome to life in paradise. It is because you loved my father that I have loved you as well. My father is still in his day of rest. So for this next 1,000 year period I will be your king and I will be assisted by 144,000 of your former inhabits that will help me accomplish my father's will of all of mankind. Thank you for sticking to me and calling Satan, my father's adversary a liar. You have all had to endure a tremendous amount of pain and suffering for me as I have for you. My father sends his tender hugs and kisses to all of you. As we move ever forward toward the fulfillment of all the promises that were foretold by prophets of old such as Daniel, Isaiah, Ezekiel and John. I want to assure you that these new scrolls will not be intrusive but will aid you in your spiritual and physical development. There will be a total of 10."

Now with the hand of man he proceeded to engrave into the stone structures the following.

1. Love Jehovah your God.
2. Love one another.
3. Respect all of creation
4. You are to be educated in the ways of the most high
5. Teach the resurrected the ways of God
6. No idols are too be used as worship of me or my father.
7. No blood is to be poured out.
8. Man and animal will live in harmony
9. Money will no longer be used. You get free give free.
10. Build and cultivate your land and homes

He then closes with joyful regards and says, "We are with you for this next 1,000 years and for forever. As you grow to perfection you will all be filled with the knowledge and strength from above that will forever bring upon you the abundance of peace and love always."

He ended that grand event with a heartwarming display coming from the heavens in the form of shooting stars that filled the sky with natural fireworks that went from one end of the earth to the other. The words "God is with you" was spelled out in the clouds. The sky was full of cheer and songs that filled the expanse of the heavens with every kind of chirping bird that sang the most beautiful symphony of joyful chirps that out did the greatest overture of Beethoven's concerto.

Another promise fulfilled found at revelation is about to be seen; revelation 22:2-3 says," and he showed me a river of waters of life, clear as crystal, flowing from the throne of God and of the lamb, (3) down the middle of its broad way. And on this side of the river and on that side there were trees of life producing crops of fruit and the leaves of the trees were for the curing of the nations.

"I cannot feel my feet, "said Jonas as he asked his father to pick him up.

"Mom I am paralyzed in this brief time period I never want to wake up form this experience. It is even better than seeing the clouds turn into chains that locked up Satan and his demons and dragged them to the abyss of Tartarus. mom, what about you?"

Flora reaches over and takes Jonas out of Dave's arms as she proceeds to kiss him all over his pudgy little face.

"That is a fact that cannot be exaggerated, "smiles Flora.
Dale, a young man that Jonas took an open shine to has come out of the cocoon of his inherited physical afflictions he had from birth. He was born with Down syndrome and was also deaf and dumb and blind. One day as he was sitting in his chair the most amazing thing happens to him.
Dales mother Pam was just about to feed him when she was thrown back on to the low armed chair she just picked herself off of. Her once withered shell of a son is now pulling himself up out of his wheel chair. His once curled up hands are opening up like a flower breaking open it's pedals, His back and head slowly lift us as if he is growing a fresh stem breaking out of the once hard soil. His body slowly starts to straighten up right in front of his mother's eyes. He then turns his head side to side and for the first time his once silent voice utters his first words ever spoken.

Dale says, "Mama, papa."

As keen scented hawks were his parents. Their breaths are hushed by the miracle of the moment. Dave uses his newly formed fully functional limbs to stand up.

His parents run to keep him from falling when he halts them and say, "Please don't help me. I want you to experience your once deaf, dumb and cripple son being release from the imperfections of the past that deprived you and dad from having a productive life. I want you to let me give back to you, even if it is just this moment. Let me walk on my own, I want to hear your once still voices. I never knew how beautiful your voices are, but I do now. I want to thank God for this opportunity to live in a world that would never have been possible if it was not for his great love for humanity."

Pam and Larry got down on their hands and knees and shouted out their praises to his great name.

They are experiencing Isaiah 11:6 where it says, "at that time the eyes of the blind ones will be opened and the very ears of the deaf ones will be unstopped."

Love is warmer than the sun that is shining on this perfect spring day. Our expressions of joy never walk but run and get swallowed up; now in the rear of time are the once lame, blind, deaf and dumb. Each day that passes the victory over their once silent voices, closed eyes, stopped up ears and lifeless limbs are now nonexistent. The seeds of joy are found like falling leaves of the agonies of the past.

Each day is a gift with the expectation of a wonderful life and forever is now a present. Another wonderful promise fulfilled, as I recall Isaiah 33:24,"No resident will say, "I am sick", the eyes of the blind ones will be open and the very ears of the deaf ones will be unstopped. At that time the lamb one will climb up just as a stag does, and the tongue of the speechless one will cry out in gladness."

There is a shattering of laughter today. Alex who never built a thing in his life attempts to hammer in a rafter on the new school we are all taking part in building. He was using the wrong side of the hammer wan an infectious virtue. He is helped to perform his task with dignity as a middle aged man named John took the hammer from his hand to show him how to use it. It was a comical moment for everyone. No insults or arbitrary condemnation are exchanged because of his lack of such a basic skill.

John hugs Alex and says," so son what did you do in your former life."

That statement struck them all to the core because they really did have a former life and never looked at it that way until John put it in such an eloquent manor.

Alex responds," I was a barber."

"Well, Alex the barber welcome to your new career we have plenty of work to do and you will be learning so much faster now that we are growing more brain cells as the days progress into years. Pretty soon we will be so smart we will need a harness to keep our brains weight in. We will need no short cuts when it comes to the intellectual vigor we are all currently starting to enjoy," said John.

Clara and Alex are always together. Dave notices how Alex gets a touch of lazy eye every time he sees Clara.

"Alex comes over here a moment," shouts Dave.

"Alex, why don't you just ask her?"

"Is it that obvious Dave," said Alex.

"Does a cat have claws? Said, Dave.

"What if she doesn't feel the same way that I do? I will never be able to be around her again.

"Come on kid. You had her at hello. Remember the first day that she meets. She told you that you have a great smile. If you want me to I can crack you on the head with a brick so that you can see straight again. She is crazy about you. Ask her the big question before Flora gets involved and you don't want that.

Dave gently shoves Alex in Clara's direction when he sees her coming their way with refreshments for the building crew.

Alex gets nervous and starts jumping up and down like he has ants in his pants.

Clara laughs and says," what are you so antsy about? Do you have to go the bathroom or something?

"No, smarty I am jumping because you make my heart feel like it is going to come out of my chest. I am jumping to keep my heart from bouncing out of my skin," replied Alex.

Clara was shocked to hear Alex make such an admission. She always had eyes for him and was a happy as a one legged man that just got his other leg back.

"I have been waiting for what seems like forever for you to ask me to be anything more than a friend to you. You had me at hello. What brought on this sudden change in you," asked Clara.

"I have always felt this way but as you know we were all too busy just trying to keep ahead of the ax that I could not ask you to be my girl. So if you don't mind can we just skip the dating stage and just marry me."

Clara picked up a rope from off of the ground and said," I will gladly tie the knot with you. All that we need now is just one more cord to make it three fold, but that one will come from God. So that being said I need not say anything else but YES.

Everyone in attendance joined in jumping for joy. We are going to have our first family wedding. Flora right away offered to make the dress. Betty offered to make the food. Kites of offers start flying. No offer was refused. We all got together to make the wedding of the century. Clara wants the wedding in a garden and that was not going to be a problem since the whole earth is picture perfect with no room for improvement needed, just love.

The garden is naturally decorated, from the lake mirrored in the ripples of love in our hearts, to the cascading waterfalls of hope forever. The gentle breeze turns the flowers into a dancing display of pink, yellow, blue, red and purple dancers of the field. The ornamental shrubs are surrounded by lady bugs, butterflies, and honeybees. Everything was perfect for this beautiful day of new beginnings. The back drop of the natural décor included the most beautiful array of Woodlyn creatures. In attendance were the white footed deer's, red squirrels, red foxes, and beavers.

The birds were on cue; as soon as Clara came into view they were to take off into full swing flapping their wings in sync arranged in 10 rows of 100 white doves. The whole area of 250 guests in attendance were surrounded by the most incredible display of exotic birds such as the cockatoos, Parrots, Amazons, and other wonderful species such as the blue Jay and 180 different song singing chorus birds, that kept the guest entertained with heartwarming song as they took to their seats.

The birds tune changes when Clara's presence is perceived. The white doves flew into action giving her the spot light.

The audience is captivated by Clara's stunning beauty. Her long dirty blonde bouncy curly hair looks as if her locks are dancing on her head. The aisle of thousands of pink and yellow rose peddles; bring out the blue in her eyes. Clara's long bridal gown has a drop waist that is not only chic, it is modest at the same time. The dress has a long, fitted torso that accents Clara's tiny waist as it cinches close to her hourglass figure. Her olive skin has natural tones of pink in her cheeks, not to mention her gorgeous bright red lips. Half way down the aisle Clara sees a lady that looks a lot like her mom. Clara has no idea who the woman is. She gets a little off ground for a brief moment and pretends that her mom is in the crowd and that is good enough for her.

Finally they face to face with each other and fall into one another's gaze of love. They join hands as they prepare to say their vows. Alex goes first. He pulls out a piece the folded up paper from his pants pocket as he nervously begins to read the words he so carefully prepared for his bride.

Alex's Vows

"You are the bone of my bone
Your voice is the sound of music that I want to hear every moment
of our lives together
You are the fullness of my being
And the complement of this man
It is with you that I have experienced
The wonders of the world of the past and future
You are the fulfillment of my dreams
It is our friendship that kept me together in time past
As we grow and learn
I keep in heart that I choose you as God has chosen us
I am your best friend and you mine
I'll am the bone of your bone
You will be the light that shine bright deep into the night
I promise you from this moment on till forever
That which God has granted us this day
Is a miracle in many a way
We came through a stormy past
To a now safe and warm existence
In paradise we will live and forever is our gift."

Flora and Dave looked at each other and said, "I never knew he could write like that."

Clara wrote her vows as well. As she wiped the tears of joy from her eyes, she begins reading.

Clara's Vows

"Today with my whole heart and soul I give to you

My love and strength
Till eternity of time
You have filled my life with joy
With laughter and smiles
My one and only one
I am your best friend and you mine
I'll be bone of your bone
You will be the light shines as long as the day is long
I promise you from this moment on and forever
Till the very end which is never
For we are now living in forever
You are my love, life and best friend
I have chosen you to be my partner for life
No woman could be prouder to be your wife
My gift from God is you
No more pain and sorrow just you and me
And bright tomorrows"

Tears of joy trickle down everyone's faces. Their beautiful sentiments linger in the air. There are no rings being exchanged just a kiss and a blessing from God up above is all that is needed. As they sealed their vows with a tender kiss a voice descends from the heavens and pronounces the following:

"Today God is granting you his blessing and from this moment on you are now man and wife. What God has put together no man will pull apart." The voice was of the king of kings himself.

Our hearts always melts like the rays of the sun melts ice in a matter of seconds. What an awesome unexpected finish to this most magnificent festival blessed by our King himself.

They had the reception on the other side of the stream. It was set up with 15 rows of handmade wood tables covered with the best silk hand woven. The bench cushions are pink cotton pillow engraved with the names "Alex & Clara Deer 8-14-2045". Each guest was to take one home as wedding keep sake. All of nature's best is at hand.

The food starts out with a classic green salad that consists of a mixture of green leaves such as watercress and spinach. A classic green salad.

The main course is a choice of creamy Alfredo pasta or steamed fresh garlic mash potatoes sprinkled with shredded cheddar cheese, both are served with roasted vegetables. There is also a large variety of breads such as sour dough rolls, croissants, and blue berry biscuits. The cake was a triple layer strawberry chocolate Oreo cookie cheesecake topped with blueberries and cherries. There was no spirits served at this ceremony the only drinks needed for the guest is dripping from the natural spring water fall. We ate so much that our clothing felt like they were about to break at the seams.

On their way home Dave and Flora realize that they were truly blessed. They are not living in a dream but living the dream.

Dave leans towards Flora and gives her playful kiss as he humbly says, "bone of my bone that was a nice touch. I would not have had it any other way my love. You are the bone of my bone I am glad we made it through to good and past times. As we grow older, but yet younger at the same time I am proud to be your husband and you my wife."

Flora replies, "amen to that baby. I love that your thick blond hair is growing back and all the wrinkles on our skin are fading away as the lines of yester-year, that are forever bygone. It is nice to see your beautiful sky blue eyes shimmer with the brightness of your youth. Not to mention the obvious that I am beginning to look like the woman you fell in love with over 25 years ago. All of my shimmers of gray hairs are turning back to luscious brown silk curves that dance on my head. I like this old to young thing that is happening to us. Jonas will never know what it is like to grow old. The fountain of youth is everywhere free for all. No plastic surgery or chemicals will ever be needed to stay this way."

They are now living in the time of psalms 113: that says," Praise Jah, you people! Offer praise, O youservants of Jehovah, Praise the name of Jehovah.[2]May Jehovah's name become blessed from now on and to time indefinite.[3]From the rising of the sun until its setting Jehovah's name is to be praised. [4]Jehovah has become high above all the nations; His glory is above the heavens. [5]Who is like Jehovah our God, Him who is making his dwelling on high? [6]He is condescending to look on heaven and earth,[7]Raising up the lowly one from the very dust; He exalts the poor one from the ash pit itself,[8]To make [him] sit with nobles, With the nobles of his people.

There is a house building project going on today for Clara and Alex's new home. There will be a total of 10 of them that are ready to break our last record of 10 hours building a house for the Clockers.

They are expecting their first child and Alex and Clara want to have their home ready for the new addition. Their friends and family have gotten together not only to challenge their former record of house building but most importantly to have things perfect for the new life that is baking inside of Clara's oven. She only has 2 weeks left and Clara is really starting to get nervous about having everything in order.

Clara and Alex have their hearts set on a 2,000 sq. ft. log cabin home. It will have four bedrooms two bathrooms with an open plan. They are thinking ahead and planning for extra rooms to accommodate Clara's family that will be coming back in the resurrection. The house will be built with just one door and window size openings so the breeze can swing in and out all day and night.

The weather never got very hot or cold. During the day it would max out around 75 degrees with a cool soft breeze. At night the temperature is about 65 degrees with the stars lighting up the sky. We did not need outside lighting the stars soft hues twinkle and toss around dim mood lighting all night. Just as Jesus demonstrated in Mark 4:39 when he told the seas to hush and be quiet and the wind abated and a great calm set in. He is now in control of the weather as well.

There is no crime so there is no need to lock your doors. No neighborhood watch, no security system and no police. They have no weapons to protect ourselves; swords were truly turned into plowshares.

The bathroom was specially designed to draw water from the hot spring that was located in their backyard. The bathtub was made out of see through glass with a matching sink and commode area.

They did not need a water treatment plant. Our water came from hot and cool springs that never got polluted. All of the furniture has already been hand crafted according to the rustic style that both Alex and Clara adored. The pieces were masculine enough for Alex and soft enough for Clara's feminine side. All of the flooring throughout the home is going to be a dark wood bamboo plank. The living room and dining room will be divided by two gorgeous wood columns that are hand peeled and stained to match the dark wood of the floors. The furniture chosen to go in the living room screams country style. The sofa and loveseat are made out of hand peeled and preserved natural Cedar wood covered in yellow, green and red pin stripped fabric that covered an eighteen inch foam that keep your bottom in a nice comfortable position.

The dining room table is made out of antique barn doors with two wooden tree stumps to secure it all. The kitchen had a matching hutch and buffet that was to be used for all of their storage needs in the kitchen. They were quite unique made with of dental molding accents with polished brass hardware and copper doors. Each room is going to be decorated in the motif of Woodland creatures. The baby's room will have a round crib that is made of Maple and Birch woods painted in olive green and beige. Clara loves frogs so she painted Lily pads and frogs on all the matching pieces of furniture such as, the changing table, dresser and the gliding rocking chair which is made in the shape of a frog. The house took a total of fifteen hours to build but it was custom to their taste so it took more time than normal.

Clara was about to give birth to their first child, that was a miracle in its self. Clara was told by a doctor in the world past that she would never be able to have a child. The day her water broke she was home alone people caring lunch for herself. Alex had gone to help build a barn for the Martins. While Clara was peeling her carrots to add to the salad that she made for lunch she felt a warm trickling down of water going down her legs. Clara knew she was about to give birth to their first child. She felt no labor pains but she knew that the baby was on its way because of the water leaking. She wanted to give birth in the natural springs on her property so she walked outside with a pair of scissors to cut the babies cord with and stood knee-deep in the water. Not more than 10 minutes after she entered the water she felt a little hand touching her leg. She looked down and saw a tiny black haired little mermaid swimming around attached to a cord. Clara used the pair of scissors to cut the cord from her baby's lifeline to her belly. Clara then walked back into the house as if nothing had just happened; it was just another day in paradise. She was overjoyed to finally meet the little cupcake that was baking in her oven for over nine months. She did not want to name the baby until her husband came home. Clara wrapped up her brand new baby in a blanket that aunt Flora made for her.

When Alex got home he sees his wife minus the bump. He goes bananas asking Clara how did she feel and can he do anything for her it was truly a water cooler moment for them. Clara asked him to please calm down so that they can both go see their resting baby girl.

Clara than says," What do you want to call our little oven warmer. I thought that we could name her Carmen. The meaning of her name says it all. It means garden in Hebrew and in Latin it means song. She is defiantly a garden song. Her beautiful thick black hair sings daddy, her cotton soft olive skin rings mama, and her mud brown eyes say garden. I say it is the perfect name for a baby born in an earth that is now restored back to the original garden that was once cut off to mankind and now fully restored."

Alex agrees and says," our future looks good wrapped up in pink knitting topped off with those beautiful bows of black curls all over her head. We did great."

"What do you mean we I don't remember you looking like a watermelon but I know what you mean. Don't worry I didn't miss the expression. I am so happy I married you and now that we have a mirror of our likeness wrapped in peaceful slumber my happiness is now complete," yawns Clara.

Clara has now come down from her 'red bull' rush of energy and is suddenly very tired. Alex tells her to take a nap; he will take care of Carmen if she wakes up.

The listening trees caught in the breeze the news of their new arrival. Within hours after Carmen was born all of their friends and family came over with gifts and food for the proud new parents. Flora brought over Clara favorite cinnamon sweet potatoes topped off with fresh handmade butter. Jonas brought over a little tree so that it could be planted in the back yard to mark the day that Carmen arrived. They all planted it together. The tree and Carmen are going to grow together and one day she is going to climb that tree. Flora was so touched by the fresh smell of baby that she decided it was time to give Jonas a sibling. They all laughed and agreed, even Jonas.

They had all just experienced the fulfillment of psalms 113: that says, "He is causing the barren woman to dwell in a house as a joyful mother of sons. Praise Jah, You people."

Alex felt as King Solomon did at Ecclesiastes 2:4-6 that reads, [4]I engaged in greater works. I built houses for myself; I planted vineyards for myself.[5]I made gardens and parks for myself, and I planted in them fruit trees of all sorts.[6]I made pools of water for myself, to irrigate with them the forest, springing up with trees.

It was the first day of summer and the new rays of sunshine beam on everything as if it has always been so. We are all united as an earthly family. One language is spoken internationally it is easy communicate with our brothers and sisters worldwide. Everything is now in perfect balance from the vegetation on the ground to the harmonious restoration between man and beast. The lion and the lamb truly live together in peace. They graze together, play together and we all enjoy each other's company which reminds me of the promise at Isaiah 65:25 where it says," the wolf and the lamb themselves will feed as one and the lion will eat straw just like the bull."

There are no more stopped up ears, or wordless voices, the once dead human limbs now join the living functioning arms and legs that take wing to flight. No more mental disorders or pills for the anxiety of life; they are things of the past that will not ever come back. No more tears of sorrow or pain those too have been erased even from memory. So whatever scared your mind and heart is no longer to come up again. Just as the bible for told in Isaiah 65:17 where it says, "for here I am creating a new heaven and a new earth; and the former things will not be called to mind; neither will they be come up into the heart."

Every day there is a large amount of empty graves being covered up and left in the dust of yester-years. No more rotting corpus. The resurrection of those asleep in Christ came out first. They are the ones that died loyal to God so therefore, they had the privilege of coming back first. We did not get to meet the faithful of old from the old testament but we planned to go the middle east real soon so that we could meet the great personalities of Job, David, Jonah, Isaiah, Daniel, Ezekiel, Abraham and Sara, the list can go on and on. We did meet faithful ones that came back from the early 1900's and they told us some very intriguing stories of their life and times.

Clara got her house ready just in time to give her mother, father and brother a nice cozy room of their own. The day they came back they were all at their house eating dinner. There was a knock at the door and we figured it was our next door neighbor's coming to join them for dinner. Clara opens the door with a plate of food in her hand. She did not say a word. We heard the plate in her hand fall and shatter on to the wood floor. Alex got up out of his chair when he heard the crash of glass.

Clara yells out, "Thank you God of love, my family is home."

Everyone gets up out of their chairs so that Clara could introduce the most precious people in her life just awaken from death.

Another wonderful promise is now being fulfilled. They are now seeing the fulfillment of acts 24:15 where it says," and I have hope towards God, which hope these men themselves also entertain that there is going to be a resurrection of both the righteous and the unrighteous."

Everyone got up to welcome them to their new world and life. It was a moment in time for all of us. When the resurrection of the righteous started they had no warning they just showed up. When the resurrection of the unrighteous took place it was a totally different experience.

"Flora do you realize that it has only been two years since the "day of wrath" has occurred; I wanted to take this time to sit with you guys and really take it all in. I want us to do a little refection of the stability and final victory over so many of life's enemies from the once common cold to how God resisted the proud and gave the humble sanctuary from our murderous former rulers to one that Subdues us with all of the virtues of humanity unprejudiced. Flora you start by giving your top 3," said Dave.

"Well, where to start I don't know if I can just do three but for the sake of fairness I believe it is best. The day that Jesus gave us the new laws is for me a pass through all the barriers of consciousness. The second is when I saw Jonas playing in the meadow with a grizzly black bear. It was like the bear was playing with a doll and Jonas was the doll. I came outside to bring them a drink and they were all on the ground fast asleep after playing so long. Rexa was sleeping in Grizzlies paw and Jonas was on his belly. Now for the final one I have to say is the day that we finish building our Victorian style home. We do not have to worry about having to pay a mortgage or oppressive land taxes. It feels great not having to worry about going to work for anyone else but ourselves. Isaiah's prophesy at Isaiah 65:22 is now fulfilled where it says, "and they will not build a house and someone else has occupancy; they will not plant and someone else does the eating, for like the days of a tree will the days of my people be. And the work of their hands my chosen people will use to the full." The ugly part of life is now made beautiful. I know that you said three but we have yet to champion the returning of a loved one asleep in death. I cannot wait to see my father again. I know you don't have any loved ones that you are waiting for but the day I see my dad again that will be the whip that creams my coffee," Flora said as she drops down on the couch and passes on the next three to Jonas.

Jonas says, "My list cannot be made because everything is new to me and I do not have the Knowledge to have wisdom. What I am most please about is the freedom from fear I like enjoy being taught by God. But most of all I love seeing all of the animals peacefully living side by side. Their lives are just as complete as ours are. I am with mom in regards to her feeling about the resurrection of the dead. I never knew grandpa and although, I want to meet him I am most interested in meeting the faithful of old characters of the bible. I know Moses is already alive again I cannot wait to go and see him and compare notes with Moses and let him know how awesome our rescue was. The parting of the Red Seas had nothing on the parting of the heavens and the chaining up of Satan and his demons as they were dragged to the abyss."

Flora and Dave are going to the beach today to catch some rays. They are waiting for Alex and Clara. Jonas had a pet shark that he always looks forward to playing with. Jonas has a special whistle that is Sharpie's cue to come out and play what he called 'fin time.' Sharpie pulls up to the waterline so Jonas can get on his back and hold on to his fin and off they jet into the ocean for "fin time."

Flora yells out to Alex to come over. Carmen loves sitting on the sand throwing what we call 'sand balls.'

Jonas came back in a lot sooner than expected. He tells us that Sharpie is acting strangely, so that was why they are back so fast. Jonas also tells his parents that while they are out he felt a sudden change in the currents. Well, not even two minutes after Jonas gets land sharked; the oceans waves rise higher by seconds. The sound of metal hitting metal is consuming our ears. They all gather together in a circle, not out of fear but out of curiosity. The sound of bells take over the crashing sound of metal and they all knew what it meant when they heard bells like that. They now know that we are witnessing a resurrection. The sea is about to give up their dead. They held each other's hands to further contain our excitement.

Jonas yells out," you guys look at the size of that ship, it is bigger than the baseball field in the park. I hope the waves that are coming our way will not wash us away.

Alex burst into laughter as he says," Everything is under control the' Dead Sea' is coming alive. So far I have counted 500 bells and they are still ringing. We will have a lot of new smiling faces to paint the town with."

The ship that popped out of the bottom of the sea had the name 'Titanic' written on the sides of the ship. They stood there with our jaws in drop position because of the disbelief of what they are witnessing. Men were waving their top hats in hand, and the women are waving their scarves and purses. All decks were full of happy spirit filled souls.

As the ship got closer someone yelled out," hello there mate, we have been out to sea for a spell and wonder where there is a good place to eat."

Alex shouted back," there is food for all, welcome back."

The beach became littered with people coming to greet loved ones. Flora saw Rachel Running to the shore line like she was looking for someone. Flora asked her who was she expecting and she told me that her great grandmother and grandfather were on that ship when it sank. I heard the bells ringing in my ears. They all know that when you hear the ringing in your ears, it was time for you to claim their prize.

My prize had a double ringing," Rachel yelled as she ran into the water calling our grandparents name.

"People are flooding the beach claiming their belongings if you know what I mean," said Flora.

The musical bells brought with them the life of times past that have come back to restore their futures sealed with a hug and a kiss from family members they never know but expected. Another wonderful promise fulfilled spoken at revelation 20:13,"and the sea gave up those dead in it and death and hades gave up those dead in them. "

They are living the fulfillment of revelation 21:4-6,"and he will wipe every tear from their eyes and death will be no more; neither will mourning nor outcry nor pain be anymore. The former things have passed away. (5) Says, "I am making all things new." (6) Says, "To anyone thirsting I will give them the fountains of the waters of the tree of life."

A week later I hear the ringing in my ears, "Could it be," Flora thought to herself.

Her heart is pumping a million miles a minute as her senses are heightened to a point of extraordinary extremes. "I smell lemons," thought flora.

Out of nowhere lemons are flying towards the house. A familiar man's voice is yelling," heads up. What will it be kid." Only one person in the whole world would say and do that, "daddy's home, "shouts Flora.

Flora and her dad Tony Maximiliano were now face to face as they ran into one another's embrase. They hug each other so inseparable that they had to hold back to catch their breath. Flora tells her dad that her life has now been too sealed in complete happiness now that he was back in her life for eternity.

The day began with a ringing and ends in the banging realization of all Gods promises are now fulfilled.

All things are restored and we will all live happily ever after or at least till the end of these 1,000 years, than the fun starts all over again. That is another story for another time because just as revelation 20:7-15 says," [7]Now as soon as the thousand years have been ended, Satan will be let loose out of his prison.

Made in the USA
Coppell, TX
17 July 2023

Wright, John, 132, 138
Wright, Mose, 289

X, Malcolm, 18–19

Zimbardo experiment (1971), 234–36
Zimbardo, Philip, 235
    ten maxims, 236–37
    torturers as "normal," 239*n*

CPSIA information can be obtained
at www.ICGtesting.com
Printed in the USA
LVOW01s0903080916
503654LV00014B/143/P